SuperHuman

SuperHuman

matt whyman

Hodder
Children's
Books

a division of Hodder Headline Limited

For Venetia

Text copyright © 2003 Matt Whyman

First published in Great Britain in 2003
by Hodder Children's Books

10 9 8 7 6 5 4

A Catalogue record for this book is available from
the British Library

ISBN 0 340 86607 1

Typeset in TimesNewRoman by Avon DataSet Ltd,
Bidford-on-Avon, Warwickshire

Printed and bound in Great Britain by
Bookmarque Ltd., Croydon, Surrey

The paper and board used in this paperback are natural recyclable
products made from wood grown in sustainable forests.
The manufacturing processes conform to the environmental
regulations of the country of origin.

Hodder Children's Books
a division of Hodder Headline Ltd
338 Euston Road
London NW1 3BH

one

An incoming squeal floods into the station, like the brakes on a runaway train. Pigeons flock to the crossbeams. They squabble for a perch in the vaults overhead, but fail to settle as the volume builds. Had anyone been present this time of night, they might wheel around in horror – only to find the tracks are lifeless, the platforms deserted and the ticket kiosks closed. No trains run until dawn but, make no mistake, an unseen force is closing in and *fast*. A shadow drops into the mix next, right there on the polished marble floor. It pools at the foot of a covered escalator – some rat run from the mall on the upper level – and that's when all hell comes flooding out.

First a figure launches from the lip of the handrail, sparking an end to that terrible sound. He's crouched on a skateboard, early teens perhaps, his arms flung outwards as he arcs into the air. The momentum from his noisy grind to ground level propels the board some distance, but he's not doing this for show. That becomes apparent when the wheels connect with the floor and a dozen or so figures flock from the escalator mouth like bats out of a cave.

'C'mon! He's ours!'

These guys are a little older, and a whole lot meaner looking. They move by rollerblade, their leather trench coats flapping noisily as they spread out after their quarry. Still he moves with a god-given grace, our boy with the board, his wheels barely touching the floor. A kick flip takes him high over a bench, buying precious seconds as the swiftest skaters are forced to swarm around it. The rear-guard goon attempts to mimic his move, only to clip the bench and fall in a sprawling heap. The collision distracts the rest of the gang, who turn to scowl and curse just a beat too long.

For when they switch back around the boy has vanished, and all they can do is glance at one another as if perhaps they have just been fooled by a ghost.

There was a time when the station operated twenty-four hours a day, but as the city became dangerously unsafe after dark, it made sense to close down at night. Nobody travelled far from home outside of daylight, after all. Not if you wanted to reach your destination with your wallet in your pocket or your heart still beating. By rights the security guards should've been here, but everyone knew they skulked home soon after locking up the last exit. They valued their own safety, after all.

Which was why the boy had headed for the guards' office, just behind the trolley storage – the office with the unmarked door and all the monitors inside. A place where he could hide.

On the screens, he has six different views of the station's interior, and that's how he can see the pack circling. They stalk the cathedral-like space in silence, rolling this way and that. He thinks of vultures waiting for their prey to let go of all hope, and tries not to breathe in case they hear him. His heart works like a jackhammer, but he can't afford to swallow, or even drop a bead of sweat. If they sniff him out it'll all be over. He might see the sun rise over the city but it won't be the same. Whatever punishment these guys choose to deliver, he knows it'll surely spell the end to his skating days, and he really doesn't need that now. Not when he's starting to find his feet.

With his board in one hand, and his back pressed to the door, he watches the monitors and waits. It's all he can do. The night is on the cusp of lifting, and if he can hold out just a little longer this crew will retreat to the other half of the city. They'll have to, for this chase started way out West from here, on their turf. Unlucky for them that the station lies on his side of the boundary line, but it just might be the break he badly needs. For the long leather coats and the blades they wear mark them out as enemy. It's the badge over there, but not here in the East. This is his territory, where anything goes so long as you're on a skateboard.

He knows that if they're spotted word will quickly spread,

which is why they look so wary as they continue to hunt him down.

So he waits and he worries for his crew . . .

Crash and Spinner had been some way behind when the ambush kicked off. It was just typical for these two to hang back in the subway sidings, getting up the finest colours that they could on all the railcars. The next morning, oh man, the whole city would see their pieces when the trains pulled through the platforms. A moving art gallery, that's how they saw it. When it came to graffiti, these guys were king, even if they had to travel far to keep their crown.

The entire crew was way out West at the time, and by rights they should've stuck together. The big guy, Marvin, and his cousin, Tiny Ti, had insisted on creeping even deeper into the network of tunnels, just to bomb the brickwork with their own ink. Enemy territory went down to the clay in this city, and at the time they were right underneath the boulevards and boutiques that made the West what it was: a place for the wealthy, with no room or time for anyone less fortunate. That's what had started this whole conflict, long before they were born, and that's why this crew had pretty much grown up with graffiti in their blood. Marking territory like this was a way of life. Unless you staked your claim then you were nothing, and being noticed in the right way is crucial to our boy on the board –

especially when it comes to the last member of this band of board-disciples.

He had taken on the rollerbladers for Katya's sake. One minute the pair of them had been whispering about how they'd like to see the suckers' faces when they found this kind of calling card, the next the suckers themselves had come out of the shadows, with all eyes on the girl. It explained why he had acted on instinct, snapping his board to hand and charging for the weakest-looking weed on wheels. It had worked, as well: the geek went down with one swing of his deck. Enraged and baying for blood, the others had promptly abandoned Kat to hunt him down.

Panic had threatened to overtake him from that moment on, but his flight instinct held true and delivered him here – to the relative safety of the monitoring room. He can barely believe he's made it right now, but it will make sense some day. Minutes earlier, down in the subway network, he had commanded every muscle in his body to deliver him home. Sprinting was never his first choice when it came to making an escape, but on that broken surface his board would have needed wings as well as wheels. The ballast bed had granted the bladers an advantage, for they could straddle the rails. As he tore on through the half darkness he had heard them closing in behind, the rumble of their wheels on the steel both steady and true. All he could do was hope and pray that the next station would soon reveal itself. Had that circle of light not appeared around a bend in the tunnel, they would have surely mown him down.

He had followed his board up on to the subway platform, slamming it there like a surfer attempting to catch a wave and landing on it belly up. Within seconds he was upright again and moving as he knew best. From there, it had been a question of speeding through the labyrinth of linked tunnels and inspection routes, even riding the roof of an eastbound freight train: anything to surface at the City Railroad Station as if his life depended on it.

Now, from his hiding place in the guards' office, he scans the banks of monitors and dares to think he might be safe. Each screen feeds a different take on the hunt going on outside that door. He almost laughs when he thinks about it, but giving away his location just wouldn't be funny so he settles for a private smile. With every angle of the station concourse covered, he can see the rollerbladers have regrouped at the foot of the covered escalator. They could be a hockey team at half time, he thinks, watching them form a circle and then revolve as one as they discuss the next option. He sees a lot of shaking of heads, and can hear them cursing his name, but that's fine by him. They'll be gone within minutes, and he'll be free to catch up with Katya and the rest of his crew. Unless, that is, one of *them* attempts to make contact with him first.

When his mobile phone begins to sing, his first response is to claw at the knapsack as if it's scalding the small of his back. He finds the phone in among all his spray paints, but doesn't shut it down. It's too late for that now. Instead, he takes the call and looks on in terror at the scene unfolding on the monitors.

'Hullo?' His voice squeaks a little, but he's too freaked out to clear his throat and try again.

'*Well, that went well.*' The boy recognises her dry, deadpan voice immediately, and the receiver burns against his ear. Even if it's the last voice that he hears before he falls to the crew now gliding ominously towards his hideaway, at least he can face them with Katya here in spirit.

'*Are you OK?*' she asks him, softening now. '*Everyone else is fine, we're almost home, but what's your position?*'

A knock at the door follows, as if to punctuate Kat's question. He frowns at the screen, for he had expected the gang to kick it open on hearing his mobile ring out. Despite feeling sick to the core, he asks her to hold on. When he opens up they're waiting for him, united by their smug grins which only rich kids from the West can muster.

'What's my position?' he repeats into the mouthpiece, his eyes locked on the ringleader. 'Not good.'

The rollerbladers begin to chuckle at this grim understatement, only to be silenced by a background squeal – the second to spill into the station in one night. They react as a pack: swivelling around smartly as if that runaway train really is coming this time. Then another shadow pools at the foot of this covered escalator, followed by three, four, five kids on skateboards. All of them recover quickly from the leap, and reform in a defiant line. This lot are dressed in radical colours: a ripped-up street punk look just like the lad who's skin they've come to save. They might be kind of young and scrawny-looking, but there's a huge guy with them, in a T-shirt that reads: **whale**. He's built like a tank on top, with short-cropped hair like he's destined for a life in the military. His shoulders are so broad, in fact, that he's able to support a boom box on one side. The way he has it pinned there with one paw, you'd think it was a permanent feature.

The other two lads don't look up to much, but the spray cans holstered on their belts confirm a unique kind of quick-draw. A couple of girls are with them, too. The really small one has her hair pulled into giant pigtails and a vicious sneer on her face. The girl beside her is dressed as if she only comes alive at night, all in black, with her raven hair and pale white skin, yet she too appears to be relishing this moment. She cups her elbow in one palm, presses a phone to her ear, and winks at the boy behind the luckless rollerbladers. This is Katya, of course.

'Lucky for you the cavalry's here,' she says. 'What would you do without us?'

He is about to protest that he could've handled this alone, – but it's too late for that now. The two sides are squaring up already.

'*Yo!*' The big guy with the buzz cut and the extra large T-shirt doesn't move when he speaks to these guys, not a single twitch. His voice seems slowed down, too, but it's certainly deep enough to command their attention. 'We can have this out, right here and now, but whatever goes down you'll never make it home.' He gestures to the station's glass frontage, at the brightening strip of sky below the stars. Dawn is creeping in at the corners of this city now, which is the last thing the rollerbladers need so far from home. 'The East is waking up, man. Always does get the sunshine first, which means any time now the bigger boys are gonna rise and wonder what that bad smell is coming outta here.'

The bladers glance at one another, looking pumped still but increasingly nervous. Behind them, our boy with the board clips out of the room, circling wide to join his crew. He is met by a furious stare from the ringleader opposite, but responds in kind as best he can. For a moment, nobody moves. It's all in the looks these two are dealing each other. The boy is clearly on edge, and blinks despite himself. For the ringleader, this is all he needs to see. He pushes back his greasy blond hair, smiling to himself. Next he lifts his fist and jabs a thumb westward. He's the first to roll as well, never letting his gaze drop as he retreats towards the glass doors. The others follow stopping only when their main man draws out a canister from the inside pocket of his trenchcoat. He shakes it briefly, tests the paint in the air, and then turns to the glass again. With his back to the skateboarders, he pumps out four slashes of black paint, but even before he steps away they know he's leaving behind his crew's trademark 'W'.

'Our card,' he says, and performs a mock bow. 'In case you've forgotten just who you're messing with here.'

'Ooh, *scary*.' This from the shorter of the two girls, the one with the outsized pigtails and the attitude. Tiny Ti, she's called, and nobody has ever needed to ask why. She blows them all a kiss goodbye, and then her face opens out in surprise. 'Look out, guys, *behind you*!'

The bladers whip around, two of them turning right into each other. They go down like clowns on banana skins, but it's egg that's left all over their faces when they find that they've been scammed. For all they find behind them are their own reflections in the glass.

The ringleader turns to glare at the girl. He's lost for words, but his expression says it all.

'Made you look,' she says with a shrug. 'One more thing, perhaps you could leave some money for all the damage you've caused?'

'It's paint,' he says. 'Leave it to the cleaners. This kind of thing keeps your people in jobs.'

'Fun-nee,' she says icily. 'I was thinking about all the glass that'll need replacing.'

The ringleader studies the fresh tag as if he's missing something. 'Why?' he asks eventually.

She presses a finger to her chin. 'Duh – it's locked?' She waits for him to test the doors for himself. 'Now, drop a couple of notes in the charity box over there, and leave in an orderly fashion.'

Even as she speaks, his face is turning crimson: a mixture of shame and rage. He debates the deal with himself, then gives the nod to his right-hand man. This guy can't believe what he's been instructed to do, but a kick to the shin soon persuades him to go fold some money into the box. Our boy with the board? He glances along his own crew, still lined up in a show of strength, and shares a look with the girl at the other end. The graffiti war will never be over but they can claim this particular conflict, one that finishes with the sound of crashing glass.

The ringleader leads the way, having built up the necessary speed by describing an arc across the marble like some kind of demon speed skater. The others follow close behind, unfolding in a spiral before snaking out into the slate grey light.

The city is on the verge of awaking, first the East and then the West.

For Katya, Crash and Spinner, Big Marvin and Tiny Ti, it's the end of another long Friday night.

For Jude Ash, the boy whose wheels have barely touched the ground, who comes alive on a board in a way that startles even him, this is only the beginning . . .

two

The Projects have been standing for a half a century now.
Even at the time of construction, these three social housing
blocks on the city's eastern fringes were nothing new.
People often dismiss them as fifty storey gravestones, even
teeth that needed pulling, but there's only one way Jude
can describe the place: *home*. He's been here all his life,
nearly fourteen years on the fourteenth floor of the central
block, with his mum and his kid brother, Sam. There used
to be another man in the family, but nobody talks about
him much nowadays.

The elevator doors creak apart, bringing warmth and
sunshine into the space. Inside, Jude and his crew blink
brightly and shield their eyes for a second or so. It's cramped
in here, but that's mostly down to Marvin. The others are
squeezed around him as best they can, and Jude almost
pops out on to the open walkway wrapped around this floor.
The others live on different levels, all of them above him.

'See you later, guys,' he says, and turns to grin at them
mischievously. 'Make sure you stay out of trouble.'

'Not a problem.' This is Tiny Ti. She's standing right in front of her big brawny cousin, waist high to the whale. You can see the connection, the hint of Hawaiian in them both, even if they're from different worlds on the physical front. Ti crosses her arms, rests her bird-like weight on one foot. 'You're the one who needs to watch your back, Jude. You made the West crew look like fools, and that's not something they'll forget in a hurry.'

Jude shrugs like he doesn't care, then considers coming clean. He's about to admit that down in the tunnels he was seriously scared, but Spinner pipes up just in time.

'Speaking of hungry,' he says, standing right beside his skate buddy, Crash. 'Who's for some sushi?'

It's Katya who pulls the first face. 'Sushi for *breakfast*? *Yeew!* I feel sick already.' She's squashed up at the back, but Marvin swiftly makes some more room just in case.

'Why not? Fresh sushi beats soggy cornflakes.'

Spinner glances at Crash for some back-up, even though his friend has never been known to talk. Most of the time, Spin speaks for him, but it's anyone's guess whether Crash ever agrees. Still, the two appear to have an understanding. Always have done. They're dressed identically, in baggy black tracksuits, gold chains and ski hats. It isn't pretty, but their wild style graffiti skills more than make up for any fashion errors.

Spinner rolls his scrawny shoulders, and says: 'Raw fish and vinegared rice is good for mind, body and soul, at any time of day. Now, I'm going to freshen up, and Crash here mos' *definitely* needs a shower. Once me and my man here are smelling sweet as I look, we'll be getting ourselves some squid sashimi.'

Katya pales visibly, while Marvin and Tiny Ti grimace like someone has dared to let one rip in this confined space. 'Cousin,' he growls, 'tell me that ain't natural.'

'Forget about fish,' says Ti, 'let's eat at your place. Your grandma does pancakes on a Saturday.'

Crash and Spinner turn hopefully to Jude, but he just shakes his head. 'The weekend's only just started,' he tells them, just as the elevator doors begin to close on his crew. 'I need some shut-eye.'

He looks at Katya, finds her pool blue eyes at the back, and immediately feels his cheeks heat up. She has a heart-shaped face and a smile that could stretch a mile wide if she wanted it to. Mostly Kat keeps a lid on that kind of look, however, using pale foundation and a sharp tongue on anyone who tried to get too close.

Five years she's been living here in The Projects: a refugee from a bigger war, somewhere overseas. Still, she learned the language soon enough, and mastered the art of sarcasm almost overnight. That she spoke with an accent that reminded everyone of murderous movie spies just served to heighten her reputation. Spinner once said that her bloodless complexion and shadow-black bob made her look like a skate punk trapped inside the body of a Goth. When Kat got wind of that, she took him to one side, had a quiet word in his ear, and Spinner never once repeated the description. Yeah, she could be pretty scary when she wanted to be, even if it was just a cover. But deep down she's the kindest person Jude has ever met. Through his eyes, Kat isn't so much the girl next door as the one from six floors up – she's on a higher level than him in more ways than one. From where he's standing right now, in fact, her presence fills the lift more than Marvin's. It means when the doors meet in the middle at last, Jude remains where he is for a moment, just thinking about her.

Thinking what a no-mark he had been: giving the game away in the subway network – right in front of her!

Jude trudges along the walkway with his board underarm. His whole body aches after the chase to the station, and only sleep will put that right. He glances westward over the balcony, towards the city scrapers. They stand in a cluster, all different heights, glittering in the early light like crystal stalagmites. Between here and there lies a vast sprawl of low-rent buildings, overhead rail tracks and billboards. Despite this early hour, the smog is beginning to thicken in the thoroughfares, so much so that Jude can't actually see the traffic that's caused it. Even the airspace is host to a scattering of low-flying aircraft, each one trailing a banner ad for something he can't afford: a grandstand seat at the rodeo, even a ticket for the weekly lottery. He figures that from the cockpits The Projects probably look like castle watchtowers – for there's nothing beyond them but wasteland. It might have been the same on the other side of the city, but nobody from round here ever dared venture that far West. All Jude knows for sure is that his own front door overlooks an endless outback of scrub and storm drains, burned-out car wrecks and weed-tangled space waste: stuff that just fell out of the sky without warning every year or so – scorched satellites past their fly-by dates and bits of booster rocket – all of it mangled beyond recognition, though the curved flanks always made good skate pipes.

Right now, a slight but freshening breeze comes off the horizon. It serves to focus Jude now he turns the corner. A wind chime hangs over his front door, tinkling gently. It's been a feature here since before he was born, strung up by one parent or another. If it ever got nicked the silence would be unnatural. Who knows? Maybe it had survived so long because the many thieves around here felt the same way. Jude finds his key and eases open the door, taking care not to add to the sound. Before padding inside, he turns for a good look out over the balcony, but it isn't just the rising sun that causes his face to light up. It's this, the East side, that *really* means something to him, and all of a sudden that chime sounds like a magic spell sailing in across the plain. For Jude, it means less people, less hassle, bigger skies and more space to skate. The West could keep its money. Cash couldn't buy the freedom he has here. The Projects may have been a dumping ground for families too far gone to fix, but just how many rich kids were dazzled from their doorsteps on a daily basis?

All is still inside the apartment. Dust motes swirl in a bar of sunshine, but that thins to nothing when Jude creeps inside and clicks the door shut. He checks his wristwatch. It's only just gone half six, so he must be safe. Everyone is still asleep. At least he thinks they are because his mother's bedroom door is closed and if Sam was awake then everyone would know about it. His little brother was the kind of kid who acted like he'd eaten way too many food additives: always fizzing over with excitement, from the moment he opened his eyes in the morning until sleep finally knocked him out at the end of the day. With no sound coming from Sam's room, however, Jude's sure he's still out for the count. He tiptoes to his own room, takes great care closing the door behind him, then breathes out long and hard. Only then does he dump his board on his bed, followed by his knapsack, his trainers, skate shorts and shirt.

All of this stuff needs to be bundled away before he climbs in between the sheets – but something draws Jude from the task at hand: the mirror on the wall.

'Oh, boy,' he says to himself. 'How embarrassing.'

He inspects his own reflection for a moment, naked but for his boxers, and then lets his shoulders fall. His face is so shiny he can almost see a reflection in his reflection. It wasn't like this when he crept out at midnight. Back then he was looking good. Well, not bad. He'd scrubbed up, twisted his jet-black hair into spikes, and then stood in this very same spot thinking tonight was the night he'd ask her out. Properly. Not just as a mate or a crew member. He and Katya had spent more time together than most, but only as friends, and now some instinct inside him was asking for more. Exactly what that meant he couldn't be sure, and it didn't help that the girl in question could bite off your head if you overstepped the mark. The whole situation was so scary and unfamiliar to Jude that all he had dared to do about it so far was look at her funny.

He glances at the photograph on the shelf below, propped there beside a bottle of aftershave, and wonders what his dad would have made of it all. It's a snap of the family: all curled up at the corners and bleached some by the sun. It was taken years ago, a time when his kid brother was just a newborn baby and they both had a father they could be proud of. That was before the booze had eased in on his life, and slowly transformed him into a shadow of a man. It wound up becoming his personal demon, one he battled with in silence for years. Finally, one evening he had just drifted out into the dark, as he always did when his thirst took a hold, and never returned again.

In this picture, however, his eyes are clear and bright, his jaw set square and his dark hair slicked back but for one rogue curl. He looks like he belongs, his dad, standing proud with his wife on one side, Jude on the other, and Sam nestled in the crook of his elbow.

Jude studies the picture for a moment, dwelling on the stories he used to hear from him back then – accounts of daring and adventure in which his father reinvented himself as the hero. Not just any hero, but a *super*hero, so he said. One who slipped out at night and staggered home in the morning with tall tales even his own son found hard to believe. Right. Nice try, Dad. Like anyone over eight is going to believe a man could flit across the city in a blink, or see in the dark like a cat on the prowl. Even then, he was worried his old man might be losing a grip on reality. If only Jude had known that he would lose a father in the process, he might have been able to help. Still, all that was in the past now – all those stupid cover stories he kept cobbling together when it was plain to see he'd been out getting hammered. Jude was the man about the house now, even if he didn't know himself some days. This prompts him to consider his reflection once again. He puffs out his pigeon chest, and says, 'Kat, do you fancy doing something together one time, y'know, on a kind of . . . date?' Then he cringes at how stupid and uncertain he sounds, and wishes she could just read his mind instead.

Finding the right moment to speak up was one thing, finding the right words was proving impossible. Jude juts out his chin for a closer inspection, thinking at the same time that his mind had been messing with his heart. He likes her. He *really* likes her, but the thoughts in his head just refuse to go public. Losing his nerve in Kat's presence was bad enough, but now his *body* seems to be in on the joke.

It isn't just his shiny face, or the skin that threatens spots – it's his voice! The way it would squeak without warning was beginning to seriously dent his confidence.

Last night, for instance, as they scoped out the sidings from a disused subway tunnel, the words coming out of his mouth had pretty much made a break for it. He and Kat had been lying on their bellies, observing the ranks of dormant rail cars. It was a time for caution, just until they could be sure there were no muggers out there, waiting for tag teams such as them. All he had done was share a quiet observation with Katya when his voice just leapt up the scale in both pitch and volume. It was so startling that Jude had clamped his hand over his mouth, as if the squeaking might continue against his will. In some ways he wished Kat had laughed about it. At least that way he could've made light of the moment with her. Instead, she had looked away to spare his blushes. What could he say to her after that? Not much, really, but then events had overtaken them when the West crew had made their presence known.

'What a night,' he says with a sigh, and focuses once more on his reflection in the mirror. 'What a muppet.'

He lifts one arm, sniffs the pit and wishes that he hadn't. Finally, and with some hesitation, he hooks a thumb inside the waistband of his boxers and peers into the gap. 'Anything *you* want to do to make life difficult for me?' he asks, flattening his lips. 'Don't pretend to be asleep down there. I know you're behind all this.'

He thinks about what he's doing here, and smiles to himself. Then he lets the band snap back just a little too smartly, and his mouth shrinks to form a perfect circle.

three

'Jude? *Jude!* C'mon on, wake up. Mum says if you're not up in five minutes she's going to confiscate your skateboard.'

This is Sam. Only ten, but with a taste for stirring up trouble that goes way beyond his years. Much as Jude loves his little brother, a wake-up call is not what he needs right now.

'What time is it?' he croaks, his lashes still meshed and sticky.

'Nine thirty,' says Sam, gleefully.

Jude groans, thinking what little sleep he's had is not going to help him seize the day too well. He can hear his mother moving around in the kitchen, clearing the breakfast in that noisy way of hers – with one ear tuned to the TV – and figures he had better put in an appearance. You did a lot of stuff like this, being in a one-parent family. For Jude, it's down to seeing just how hard his mum has to work to keep them housed, fed and watered. She holds down a typing job at City Hall by day, and an evening shift in the local laundry, even though her full-time occupation is to worry endlessly about her sons. She had been there for Jude when he got bullied about his dad at school, and he'd even seen her stand her ground when six heavies turned up to repossess the sofa and the television. Then there's the food parcel she prepared every day for the old man at the top of the block. All these family commitments, and she still had time to look after others. *That* was why Jude always made an effort with his mother, even little things like surfacing before she left for work. It was a simple matter of respect. If she knew that her son had been out tagging all night she'd freak on the spot, but Jude is confident that would never happen. Every evening she goes to bed exhausted, unlikely to wake unless the place is on fire, and that gives him all the freedom he needs. With this in mind, Jude forces himself out of bed and into his clothes. Yep, he thinks, as Sam turns to lead the way, there are a lot of breaks to be had in a broken home, no matter how much he hated that word.

'About time, mister! Is there something you want to tell me?'

She says this without actually turning from the sink to face him. It's an eyes-in-the-back-of-the-head routine that once kept the boys in check. There was a time when Jude would crumble when his mum quizzed him in this way. In the past, he'd confess to small-time stuff like not tidying up his room or forgetting to buy the milk, but lately he'd grown wise to the fact that she was basically calling his bluff. Jude knows she has no reason to suspect he's been out half the night, and that's how it'll stay unless he's dumb enough to answer her question honestly. Which is why he reaches up for the cereal box, stored in the cupboard above the sink, and dares to use her shoulder to gain that extra inch. 'All I can say is that we couldn't manage without you, Mum. You're the man, so to speak.'

He comes down off his tiptoes to face her, grinning now, and in response gets a playful slap around the chops with a wet dishcloth. She's a broad woman, Jude's mum, but always knows how to dress so it looks good on her. Over the years her long hair has turned grey, but she still wears it pulled back in a pony-tail, just as she did in the photos Jude has seen of her as a carefree teenager.

'I have to be at work in half an hour,' she says next. 'Can I trust you to look after your little brother today?'

'*Yay!*' Across the room, Sam punches the air.

'But Mum, it's Saturday!'

'Tell me about it,' she says, returning to the dishes. 'I haven't had a day off in a fortnight now, but we need the money, Jude. We really do.'

Jude glances at his kid brother, feeling for both of them now, and places the cereal box on the table. Then he turns to the sink, takes the cloth from her hand, and says, 'I'll finish the dishes, and don't worry about Sam. It's about time I showed him how to ride a skateboard properly.' She faces him now, both eyes shining, and for a moment he thinks she might cry. It's something she comes close to doing a lot, without actually shedding a tear. Occasionally, Jude wishes she would let it all go, just rant and rave about her lot in life instead of pretending she can cope. Still, that's not what she wants to hear right now.

'We'll be fine,' he says, awkwardly. 'We always do OK.'

She smiles, but says nothing. There's no need. Her expression says it all, though that fades as the city news cuts from the studio to an outside broadcast. Jude glances at the miniature screen, stationed on the hatch between the kitchen and the front room. It's one of those old school TV/radio things he had found abandoned in the wasteland and cleaned up back home. Just then, however, he wishes he had left it for the weeds to claim, all tangled as it was in toadflax at the time, because the report is focused on the City Railroad Station. The newshound is standing in front of the smashed glass entrance, a familiar figure alongside.

'*Marshal Dawe*,' the reporter bleats, '*what can be done to halt the increasing turf war between these so-called graffiti gangs—*'

'Can't we watch cartoons?' Sam appeals to his brother, but Jude keeps his eyes fixed on the screen. Watching the reporter finish the question, he prays his mother won't make the connection.

'Leave it,' he says. 'Let's hear what Dawe has to say.'

'*This is a problem that stems from the East side,*' the Marshal begins, causing Jude to bite down on his tongue, '*but it's an issue for the city as a whole, and I intend to stamp it out. These vandals are a product of that neighbourhood. They're raised in poverty, and thrive on petty jealousy, but all that will change from this day forth. We're here because I'm delighted to take this opportunity to announce a new regeneration project! One that will mirror the splendour and prosperity enjoyed by the West . . .*'

'Oh, great,' Jude's mother sighs. Working as she does at City Hall, this man is also her paymaster. 'That means more paperwork for me – though I guess it guarantees more overtime.'

Marshal J Dawe was larger than life in more ways than one: a big figure who always dressed in his tasselled suit, shoelace tie and ten-gallon hat. He had traded on this cowboy look since taking the mayoral office as a young man, even going so far as to outlaw the position of Mayor and establish himself as Marshal. This city was threatening to become run down and lawless, so he declared on first being elected so many years ago. As a result, he had gone on, the man in charge needed a job description that didn't make him sound like a powerless sissy, good for nothing but opening ceremonies and church events. It was in his role as the 'Marshal' that Dawe had pledged to clean up the city from top to bottom. Everyone really believed this man who never stopped beaming could make a difference, and indeed he had. It was just only one side of the city ever seemed to benefit. The West had truly prospered, while the East was left to crumble and decay. But hey, the people over there really mattered to the Marshal: namely the majority of voters he could always count on, plus friends and family – and there were a lot of those in high places.

'. . . *we have big plans for the impoverished, far eastern districts, but mark my words*,' the Marshal says to finish, turning briefly to the pool of broken glass behind him and then coming back to wag his finger at the camera, '*there will be no more room in this city for vandals. When we track down those responsible, they will be sorely punished*.'

'Quite right,' says Jude under his breath. 'Why don't you start the investigation a little closer to home?'

'What was that?'

'Nothing, Mum.' Jude returns to the washing up. 'It's just Dawe talks out of his ass—'

'Language!'

'Well, it's true. What's the betting this so-called regeneration scheme is a cover for something less desirable?'

'You never know, he transformed City Hall pretty good.'

'Well, he certainly transformed *part* of it,' says Jude,

finishing the final plate. 'We all know what he had fitted to the very top of that building.'

'A big glass dome,' Sam chips in. He shuts down the TV, and stands in front of the screen like he's the one before the camera. 'A dome with a *panoptic* view. I read that some place. It means the Marshal can see all over the city: North, South, East and West. The idea is that people behave themselves because there's a chance he might be watching!'

'Thank you for that, Sam.' Their mother sighs. Her youngest son is as smart as he is excitable. 'I do work there.'

'No, you work in the basement, Mum. With the dodgy heating and the paint peeling off the walls. It's Dawe who spends his day up in the clouds, looking out over the city like he created it or something.' Jude pauses just there, and accepts that he's a little too fired up for his own liking. Even his mum is looking at him strangely.

'Why can't you be this passionate about your schoolbooks?' she asks.

'Because schoolbooks aren't corrupt to the core,' says Jude, and that's when she gives him this look. It's something he's never seen before, but he feels her gaze reaching deep inside him.

She presses a palm to his cheek, and smiles. 'You're so like your dad,' she says. 'Just don't let your sense of right and wrong get the better of you, too.'

Jude's phone beeps from the bedroom just then, signalling the arrival of a text message. It's also a prompt for Sam to race for the handset before Jude can get there. He grabs it from Jude's bedroom, comes out reading the name on the screen with a big grin all over his face. 'Guess who it's from?'

Jude flinches, not least because he knows full well that Katya will be behind it. He still hasn't got his head around how much easier he finds it texting her instead of talking. Over recent months, a hint of flirting even crept into the friendly banter, but whenever Jude tries to repeat it in the real world things just become too intense. Right now, however, that message means more to him than life itself. He fixes Sam with a cold, hard glare, and shows him an upturned palm.

'Sam,' his mother snaps. 'Hand it over, right now. Your brother's in charge today, remember? Do what he says, or you'll have to come to work with me for the day.'

Sam's grin begins to shrink, the joke not funny any more. Begrudgingly, he hands the phone over. 'I can't see why you don't just ask her out,' he tells Jude. 'What's the big deal anyhow?'

Jude takes the mobile, says: 'Let's talk about that in a couple of years, see if it's so easy for you then.'

'Well,' Sam says, and that grin begins to return, 'if you'd like *me* to ask her out for you, just say the word.'

Jude ignores him, and checks the message.

Rise n shine! Meet me @ the buckled fence - XK

'I have to go,' he says, turning for his bedroom to collect his board and knapsack. 'I'll grab some breakfast later.'

'Not so fast, hotshot.' His mum gestures at Sam. He's standing there with his brow hitched high. 'Aren't you forgetting someone?'

Jude sighs, motions his kid brother to join him, and then reaches high to catch the food parcel that his mother slings his way.

'Take this up to Benjamin, when you're done,' she tells him.

He doesn't need to ask what's inside the brown paper wrapping. It's the same every day. The old man in question only ever eats honey sandwiches. Right now Jude's so hungry, he wonders if he'll be able to resist them himself. It's only when he glances up to say goodbye that a second package arcs towards him.

'I knew you'd skip breakfast,' she says, and folds her arms in mock annoyance.

'Thanks, Mum.'

'What can I say? *Someone* has to look out for you.'

four

Katya stands with her hands on hips, her head tilted up to the sun. She's wearing a capped black T-shirt with lots of bangles on both wrists, and skate-torn jeans with a studded belt. Where Jude's own clothes always seem to hang off his frame, her outfit hugs her figure in a way he can't stop thinking about. Jude catches sight of her just as soon as he hits the last flight of steps out of the block. He's on his board once more, with his little brother jogging close behind. Kat has her back to The Projects, facing the high chain-link fence that was supposed to stop you getting into the wasteland beyond. At first glance, it looks impassable. Coils of razor wire cap off the top, snagged with burst balloons and carrier bags, but you only had to root around to find the ragged holes and the tunnels. Nobody guarded this perimeter, as such. If they did, it would feel like a prison, even if it had been erected years ago to keep the scavengers from coming in. Katya turns as the boys cross the parking lot. As she does so the light catches the silver crucifix around her neck, momentarily dazzling them both.

'Well, *hello*,' Sam purrs, much to Jude's embarrassment. 'You're looking good.'

'Why, thank you.'

Sam jabs his older brother in the ribs, says: 'Doesn't she look *great*?' and receives a sharper jab in return.

'Ignore him,' says Jude apologetically, even though he totally agrees with his brother. 'I got your wake-up call. What's up?'

'This.' Katya steps to one side.

'Oh no.'

The notice has been wired to the fence, sandwiched between two Perspex plates. The type is so small Jude has to move in close to read it: 'Land acquired by *Cactus Industries*, by order of the Marshal . . .' He trails off and scans to the last full stop. 'They're building a recycling plant. Work starts . . . middle of next week!'

'They can't,' pleads Sam, despite never venturing beyond this boundary line, by order of his mum. 'Can they?'

'If Dawe is behind it,' Jude says, 'they can probably do anything they like.'

'Oh yeah?' Katya tips her head back defiantly. She shoots a thumb over one shoulder. 'Bet they can't pull a Spin Jam Slam on the storm drain in there.'

Jude shifts his focus through the chain link to the drain in question, reflecting on the trick that Kat has just described. It was in this sunken concrete half pipe that Jude first found his balance on a board, and progressed to earn his skate wings. Oh man, that was the *bomb*: the heart-stopping point when the wheels left the lip of the drain and you climbed into the sky. No matter how much air you grabbed before coming back down to earth, there was nothing like it. And if Marshal Dawe had his way, there'd be nothing like it any more.

'What can we do?' he asks. 'I guess a recycling plant can only be a good thing for the area.'

'Good for employment. Good for the environment. Good for the local people?' She stops there to let him think about it. Then: 'Jude, this is *Dawe* we're talking about here. The man never does anything unless it's good for *him*. Now, I'm not going to stand back and let the bulldozers clear our patch until I know all the facts behind the project, but I need some support here.'

'I'm in!' Sam salutes Kat, but she continues to look at Jude, holding out for an answer. Jude glances one more time at the long grass and the burned-out cars, sights a bird of prey hovering high overhead. Then he reaches back for his knapsack, and draws out one of his spray cans. He flips off the lid, and then slashes the notice with a lime green tag. 'Just in case people think we're going to take this lying down,' he says, standing back to admire his work.

'Never say die!' declares Sam, and attempts an appreciative finger snap that serves only to hurt him.

Nursing two fingers, he looks up at his brother and says, 'So, what are we going to do, exactly?'

Jude turns to Kat, feeling no sense of awkwardness or hesitation in her presence, just as it used to be. This isn't about him, after all. This is about everyone in the crew.

'We need the lowdown on Cactus Industries,' he tells her.

'Better leave it to me and Tiny Ti, then,' she says. 'We'll see what we can find online.'

'Are you going to hack their system?' Sam seems set to explode with excitement. Everyone knows that when the girls get in front of a keyboard they're like witches with a spell-book. Some of the coding tricks they could pull in cyberspace just took your breath away. 'Can I help, Kat? *Please.*'

'You don't need to be a hacker to gain information from the Internet,' she says, and flattens her scarlet-painted lips. She always looks pained like this when people praise her code-cracking skills. 'It's just a question of knowing where to look.'

'If you want to make yourself useful,' Jude instructs his little brother, 'go tell Ti to fire up her computer, then put the word out to the rest of the crew – have them be here at sundown.'

'That would make me the runner,' Sam protests. 'I can do better than that.'

'You can have my role if you like,' says Jude.

'Yeah?' Sam brightens now. 'What is it?'

Jude reminds him of the brown paper bag inside his knapsack. 'Sandwich delivery boy,' he says, and winks at Kat when his brother declines the offer. Then he stamps on the tail of his skateboard and catches the nose when it flips into his reach. 'I won't be needing this where I'm going,' he says. 'I was thinking one of you could look after it.'

'Don't look at me,' says Kat, who can see where Jude is heading. 'I don't need wheels to surf the net.'

'Go on then,' Sam offers, trying hard to keep his cool. 'I guess I can help you out.'

'OK, but stay out of trouble. Any problems, call the man upstairs.'

Benjamin Three-Sixty inhabits the top floor of Jude's block. Strictly speaking, it isn't a floor at all, but the roof. If you want to gain access, you have to take the elevator as far as it'll go, then climb the fire escape from the highest balcony – the one with nothing above it but blue sky. You wouldn't go far if you fell; the ladder was housed inside a cylindrical cage to insure against that kind of horror. Even so, whenever Jude makes this climb he breaks out in a cold sweat. Sure, the view over his shoulder might be spectacular, but he's happy to accept that as a fact without actually checking it out for himself. As he reaches the summit, he finds what can only be described as a shack occupying the centre of the roof. With a sloping tin roof, chicken wire fencing and a worn wooden stoop, it would look more at home on a roadside than a rooftop, but it's been here so long that The Projects could've been built underneath – lifting it to this lofty height. Most probably a lot of people didn't even know it existed. From the ground, all you could see was the giant satellite dish behind it. Officially, this hulking great receiver exists to feed every block with television signals, but the fact that someone has spray painted CHANNEL ZERO across the pan suggests another use, as does the tell-tale cable that snakes out to join it from the shack's tin can chimney.

Jude climbs on to the roof of the block, wishing the wind would stop buffeting so badly, and moves towards the shack. There's a zinc-top table and a couple of rocking chairs on the stoop. Sometimes he finds Benjamin out here, sipping lime cordial through a straw and just watching the world below. Today, Jude has to knock on the door to make his presence known. He gives it a couple of thumps, and then stands well back. He waits, almost a minute, but just as he's about to try again the door crashes outwards. With it comes the sound of music: drum and bass cranked up loud and loose. The inside of the door is clad in foam and egg boxes, soundproofing put in place by the elderly Rastafarian with the waist-length dreadlocks, now looming large on the stoop.

'Hey, Ben.' Jude waits for the old man to register who he is, and then shows him the wrapped package. 'It's sandwich time.'

'Mmm, *mmm*, sweet honey,' he says at last, and promptly retreats inside the shack. 'Bring yourself in,' he calls back. 'I'm on air!'

Jude follows him inside, wondering at the same time if Benjamin ever *stopped* broadcasting. Every time he comes up here, the man is in front of his microphone. Anyone who ever tuned into his pirate radio station claimed he worked right round the clock, which is what had earned him the surname of Three-Sixty. The man went full sweep, after all.

'Have a seat,' Ben says, and gestures to the plastic chair on the opposite side of his mixing desk. Jude stays where he is for a moment, watching the DJ at work. He pops a vinyl record from its sleeve, flips it on to one of three spinning decks, then closes in on the fader and the drop microphone hanging in front of his nose.

'Ooooh,' he crows, 'howbout *dat*!' Benjamin's street-smart links could often make Jude cringe. It just didn't sound right from a man his age, but then it came from the heart, and that was what really mattered. 'Original sound comin' atcha from Channel Zero,' Ben continues, his voice cutting over the beats, 'with respect doo to the East Crew. You know who you are and we know you bin busy *ripping* it up 'cross town, spreading the good word to our neighbours out West. You the Zero heroes, my friends! So wherever you are, whatever you're doing, this next wax has your name etched on every blessed groove.' There's no full stop, no pause for breath, just a teeth shaking *boom* as Ben brings in the next track. Then he snaps off the studio speakers, and appears to relish the silence. He flops back into his seat, almost creaking as he goes, and suddenly looks to Jude like a man who deserves his pensioner's travel pass.

'I heard about the wasteland,' he says with a sigh. His voice is very different now: all slowed down and slightly sad. 'It's an awful shame to lose that space.'

'It hasn't happened yet,' says Jude, sounding less sure of himself this time. 'I just don't know how we can stop it. I mean, who's going to listen to a bunch of kids feeling sore about losing their skate park?'

'You'll find a way.' Benjamin Three-Sixty opens up his sandwiches, watching Jude chew on his own. 'You done something with your hair?' he asks next, squinting some. 'What's with the spikes?'

'It's been like this for a few months now.' Jude senses his scalp tighten with all the attention it's suddenly getting. He's been coming here with the daily sandwiches since he was in shorts: has done ever since his dad left, in fact.

Ben was a good friend to his father, and over the years the old recluse had become a friend to him too. It was only recently, however, that Jude had switched into low-slung skate pants, and become more aware of his appearance, but this is the first time Ben had mentioned it. *If he's only just noticed*, Jude thinks, *then he must be getting on*. Still, he covers quickly by saying, 'I felt like a change, that's all.'

'It's called growing up.' Ben chuckles to himself, and pushes his hand through his own rope-like tresses. 'I do wonder when that stage ever ends.'

Jude hears him out, but his thoughts have drifted, not just to the wasteland this time, but how it is between him and Kat. 'Sometimes I just wish I was older,' he says. 'At least then I could handle stuff better.'

'It'll come in time,' Ben advises. 'Then you reach an age where you start to wishing you was younger, but ain't nothing you can do about that.' They share a faint smile, only Ben's grows a little sly at the edges. 'This is about a girl,' he says. 'Isn't it?'

'No,' Jude replies, just a little too quickly. When he looks back across the table, Benjamin is still there: holding out for a better response. 'All right, maybe it is.'

'I knew it,' he says. 'And is she as sweet on you?'

'If only I could be sure.'

'So, that gives you two choices.' Ben turns to the bank of

vinyl stacked on shelves behind him. He selects a disc, flips it over and over between his fingers, then lets it fall cleanly on to the next turntable. 'First up, you can make your interest known to this little lady. I mean, really go for it so she's in no doubt about the way you feel.'

'And then what?'

'Ignore her.'

Jude takes a moment to digest this.

'I can't do that,' he says finally. 'Going hot and cold is just childish.'

'Indeed,' says Ben, listening to the track on air through one side of his headphones. 'Sadly, it's what a lot of boys would do in your shoes. That kind of bad behaviour guarantees a reaction from the person they like and leaves them feeling in control.'

'It wouldn't leave me feeling very good about myself,' Jude admits. 'Besides, this girl is not someone you want to cross.'

'Which leaves you just the grown-up option.'

'And that is?'

'*Ask her out*, dumbass!'

He sighs, having held out for a second that Ben was about to share a more surefire means of winning a date. 'You make it sound easy,' he says, 'but last time I tried it all went wrong just as soon as I opened my mouth. I'm almost too scared to try again.'

Ben considers Jude for a moment, sizing him up, it seems. Then he springs forward in his chair, as if the advice he has to offer is going to be his only option. 'Dating is like skating,' he declares. 'On a board, you're always thinking two tricks ahead, right?'

Jude considers this, and begins to nod. 'I guess it's something you do without thinking, but yeah, you're right. It's important for the flow.'

'Just as it is when approaching chicks for a date.' Ben spreads his palms. 'You gotta plan two steps ahead and see them both through, no matter what. Even if it leaves you looking like a damn fool, at least you gave it your best shot.'

Jude is reminded of the last time he drew breath to see if Kat fancied doing something without the others in tow, and it prompts him to draw his phone from his pocket. He runs his thumb across the screen, still thinking things through. Finally, he looks up at Ben, and says: 'Do you reckon it would be OK to ask her out by text message?'

five

It takes a good few minutes to return to ground level from **CHANNEL ZERO** and that's just by the creaky old elevator. Jude prefers to take the stairs, not because it's safer that way, but for the simple reason that an audience with Benjamin Three-Sixty tends to leave him in need of some time and space to himself. After every visit, it's the memory of his father that trails him back down the fire escape. Ben was a close friend of his dad's, after all, but what really brings it home is how they both lived with their heads in the clouds. The big difference between the two men was that people respected what the doddery DJ did with his life. Ben may have been eccentric, but he didn't try to fool anybody. Did his father really think people would believe he was out every night saving this city from corrupt forces? *C'mon.* Maybe that's why he reserved his tales for those too young to know any better. It was humiliating to think that as a lad he had swallowed every word. Either his old man was laughing on the inside whenever he launched into another story, or he had genuinely fooled himself.

Damn you, Dad, Jude thinks to himself. *What kind of hero pulls a stunt like that?*

As soon as he was old enough to know the difference between fantasy and reality, Jude's view of his dad had darkened considerably. Worse still, he knew that soon it would be Sam's turn to grow wise to the fact that the guy had been a liar as well as a lush. Yeah, his kid brother had heard all the stories just as he had. As small boys, they would actually look forward to the moment his dad drifted home and reeled out another yarn that somehow justified his absence. By the time Jude had grown up enough to question the truth behind the tales, his old man was long gone.

He had disappeared from their lives years ago now. Just taken off without a word of explanation. Into his own dream world, most probably. Nowadays, when Jude had something on his mind, he opened up to Benjamin. The old DJ was good with homework problems, and advice on keeping his mum sweet, but Jude always tended to stop short when it came to the personal stuff. This morning was the first time he'd talked to Ben about girls, and that was embarrassing enough. Had his father still been around, Jude wonders if it would've been easier talking to him about the way his mind and body seemed to be switching on to different things. His old man certainly had no problem talking about his *own* daily transformations. Jude can almost hear his deep, sandpapery voice as he trudges down flight after flight – heading back to earth.

It happens near dark, he would begin, his breath always soured by way too much whisky. *I feel an energy coursing through me, son. It crackles through my bones, makes me feel invincible, and the only way I can live with that kind of calling is by watching over this city until the next sun rises. Let me tell you about the time I stopped a robbery that would've stripped every citizen of their entire life savings . . .*

. . . and so he would spin yet another legendary tale of selfless bravery and heroism that seemed so impressive at the time. It was only when Jude dared to take it to his mum that she laughed bitterly and explained that the only calling the man ever answered was one that took him to the bars downtown. OK, so he wasn't a violent kind of drunk. If anything, his problem with alcohol just made him seem a little lost, but that didn't stop the lies from packing the biggest punch of all.

Jude wonders how his dad would react if he knew about the changes planned for the wasteland. If he were still around today, would he offer to stand firm at the gates and stop bulldozers with one hand until the plans had been properly investigated? It was the kind of line Jude could imagine his old man coming up with. Even if, in reality, he would have been fit for nothing more than finding a nice car wreck to sit in so he could get blitzed on the sly.

Winding his way down the stairs now, feeling both distracted and a little dispirited, Jude half wonders what it would be like to run away from his own problems. With what feels like the weight of the world on his shoulders, there is something very tempting in the prospect of just climbing on to his skateboard and riding for the horizon. Then again, he knows all about the grief that kind of behaviour causes to those left behind, plus he'd most probably be homesick in no time. This is his world, after all, and when Jude considers all his friends and family, not to mention the girl who lights up his life, he figures his only option is to take the old DJ's advice and make the most of it.

The wasteland is the best place to be when the sun goes down over the city. Once that molten orb drops behind The Projects, the light just detonates between the blocks. You couldn't even look that way if you wanted to, though Marvin has more immediate things to take his breath away. This evening, he's sitting on the lip of the half pipe, his squat legs dangling over the drop, watching a figure blast out of the pipe on the other side and then loop around with nothing but the big sky behind him. Marvin knows all the trick terms: from crooked grinds to nosegrabs, fastplants, fakies, even backslide disasters, but right now all that matters is what he's seeing here – it's just beautiful to watch.

'Aim higher, Jude!' he booms, in competition with the beat box beside him. It's pumping out a trance track, a bid to keep his friend focused. 'Really push it this time!'

In response, the boy on the board hurtles back across the floor of the drain, dodging a shopping trolley that has found its way down there. He climbs the incline, and switches into the air just away to the big guy's right. It causes Marvin to duck and swear at him, only to whoop and clap when the wheels reconnect with the concrete to his left.

'Over my head and out of sight!' he yells. 'Man, you are *dope*.' Heaving himself around now, Marvin calls out across the scrub. 'Yo, squirt, you gotta check out your big brother!' Sam occupies a cracked concrete basin just behind the drain. He's borrowed Marvin's board so he can practise some of the basic tricks that Jude has been showing him all afternoon – stuff like how to kick the board from a standstill so it flips into your grip, and not smack into your face like it does now that Marvin has distracted him.

'What did he do?' Sam sounds a little dazed as he struggles back on to his feet.

'You missed it? That's too bad.' He faces back to the half pipe, where Jude continues to plunge and climb. 'It means nobody's gonna believe me when I talk you up, Jude. Shame the others aren't here to see it for themselves.'

'They're on their way,' grunts Jude, and drives his board back down the facing slope.

Marvin turns towards The Projects. He twists from the waist as he always does, as if his neck is just too wide to go it alone. 'Where?' he asks, shielding his face with his palm turned outwards. 'I can't see nothin' but sunshine.'

'They're coming.' Jude sweeps across the floor of the pipe, momentarily disappearing from view as he hits the steep ascent. 'I feel it.'

This time the jump leaves Marvin speechless. All he can do is watch bug-eyed as his buddy explodes into the boundless blue. Jude grabs the edge of his deck and takes it through a full rotation, but something doesn't play out as it should. He just seems to hang there for a second too long, almost turning out of time with the rest of the world.

The big guy doesn't blink when Jude reconnects with the slope. All Marvin can do is watch him grind to a halt before snapping off the beat box and jabbing one fat finger at him. 'How d'you do that?' he asks. 'With wings or some kinda string?'

In the wake of what's just happened, Jude can only look up at his friend from the base of the drain and share in his astonishment.

'Trick of the light?' he offers weakly, and turns to face the glare.

Marvin attempts to look towards The Projects once more as well, squinting hard to combat the shimmer and dazzle. This time, he makes out movement over the long grass, just in front of the fence. It's the crew, cast in silhouette as they walk towards them. He locks back on Jude, and then appears to remind himself to speak. 'How could you see them coming?' he asks, pointing their way across his barrel chest. 'Jude, you freak me out sometimes.'

I just freaked myself out, Jude thinks, and scrambles from the pipe. First of all, he really *had* sensed that the crew were close by. Katya in particular. Maybe it was the trance track playing mind games with his head, but he had picked up on the vibe so clearly he could've been some kind of human antenna. It was only when he had launched himself from the lip of the drain that he tuned back into the aerial stunt in mind, and what in God's name happened there? Turning the board through the air was a challenge, but standard issue if you put your heart and soul into it. This time, as he hurled himself into the manoeuvre, Jude had experienced what could only be described as an upward force. The charge had rushed through his feet, *bursting* into every fibre of his being. It was an electric moment, quite literally gravity defying, and just before it faded out his capabilities had suddenly seemed limitless. Then the wheels had reconnected with the concrete, and it all seemed like a dream. Had Marvin not gone on about what just occurred, Jude might've dismissed it as just that. A dream. Never to be repeated.

'You're gonna have to bust that move again,' the big guy tells him. 'So they can see it with their own eyes.'

Jude pretends not to hear, and whistles for his brother to come across. He still feels wired, but bewildered as well and reluctant to break it down with Marvin. Not now Katya is walking towards him with Crash, Spinner and Tiny Ti. It had been bad enough when his voice broke up in front of her. The last thing he needs right now is for Marvin to keep up the fuss and leave him feeling even more uncomfortable in her presence.

'Hey, Kat,' he calls out instead, anxious to move on. 'What did the web serve up on the Cactus Industries deal?'

She shrugs and swaps a look with Tiny Ti. 'Nothing in the newsgroups, I'm afraid, and even less on the bulletin boards.'

'The only freely available info was on their website,' adds Tiny Ti, 'but it's just press releases, the stuff they want you to see.' She stops there, as if too ashamed to continue.

'Guys,' said Kat, stepping forward now. 'We gave it our best shot, but a girl can only be in front of a screen for so long before she has to do some online shopping.'

'It's the sale season,' says Ti, apologetically. 'We needed shoes.'

Jude tries hard not to look disappointed, but it's too much for Tiny Ti. As she begins to giggle, a great big grin breaks out across Kat's face. She shows him the print out rolled in her hand. 'C'mon, did you really think we'd give up to go *browsing*? Surely you know me better than that!'

Jude feels his cheeks colour, and from where he's standing in this circle of friends *everyone* seems to notice. Crash and Spinner pop a glance at each another, as do Marvin and Tiny Ti. Even Sam is looking at him knowingly, he thinks, so it's a relief when Katya puts him out of his misery by handing him the document. Jude snaps it open. He buries his gaze into the text, but his focus is all shot now. He wishes the others would just give him a moment, if only so he can ask her out and get it over and done with. She'll say no, he's sure, but at least then he could concentrate on the task in hand.

'Sooooo,' says Spinner, stringing out the question because Jude is just staring blankly at the sheet. 'Are you going to read it out to us, or do you want some help with the big words?'

'It's a list,' Jude says, recovering now. 'A list of names.' He looks at Kat for an explanation, aware of the playful smile still lingering at the corners of her mouth.

'You're looking at all the shareholders in Cactus Industries,' she tells them. 'These are the people behind the venture, the ones who put in a little money and hope for a big return.'

'Anyone we know on there?' asks Marvin, looming over his cousin. 'If Marshal Dawe is a backer then we're home and dry. He's supposed to work for the benefit of this city, not his bank balance.'

Jude shakes his head. 'There's no Dawe on here. Just a bunch of fat cats.'

'Yep, but what's interesting is that one of the names on the list is a company, and it owns a lot of shares. See there? *Sheriff Holdings*.' Kat's finger appears over the top of the sheet to tap on the name in question. 'For a man who styles himself as a cowboy, don't you think that's a bit of a coincidence?'

Jude looks to Crash, then Spinner, Sam and Marvin. Tiny Ti just offers them a shrug, as if she's yet to be convinced herself. Now it's Katya's turn to feel all eyes upon her. She sighs heavily like a teacher before a class of nitwits, and says, 'Marshal Dawe likes to make out that he rode into the city with a mission to clean it up, right? That's what the ten-gallon hat is all about, even if his image is just a cover because we all know the man is basically a crook. So, when I see there's a Sheriff Holdings on the list, I start to think maybe there's a connection.'

'Did you find out by hacking into the Marshal's computer?' asks Sam, overwhelmed once again by the thought that he's now in the presence of a master cyber-mind. He shifts his feather-like weight from foot to foot, desperate for details, only to deflate on the spot when Kat explains how she did it.

'I looked in the phone directory, actually. But there isn't a single Sheriff in town, so to speak.'

'Kat even got me to check if the company has been officially licensed to trade,' Tiny Ti chips in, 'but apparently the entry is too recent and still being processed.'

'Which is when I began to smell a rat.'

'Or a mouse,' says Spinner, and beams at Katya like she'd just missed out on the perfect punch line. The Crew remain silent, however, plainly irritated by this needless interruption. 'A computer mouse?' he's forced to explain. 'Gedditt?'

'Spin,' says Marvin. 'Shut up and let the girl finish. It'll be no laughing matter if we lose this wasteland. Not least because you need more skating practice than most.'

Spinner shrinks from Marvin's gaze, and looks to Crash for support. They might appear identical in their ski hats and baggy wear, but everyone knew the difference between the two lads by the way they communicated: Spinner was all mouth, while his buddy preferred to stay silent and let his body language speak for him. Like now, when Spin repeats his mouse gag and receives a clip round the back of the head from his friend. Just enough to tip his hat over his eyes and cause everyone to fall about laughing.

'Enough already!' Spinner grapples with his headwear. 'I'm only trying to be funny because it doesn't seem like we have much else to smile about.' He addresses Kat directly now, says: 'All we have is a suspect name. What are we going to do about it?'

Katya winks at Jude's kid brother, says, 'We're going to take a look at Dawe's computer. See if he's left his files undone, so to speak. If we can link him to this Sheriff Holdings then that's pretty much all the evidence we need to save the wasteland.'

'Great,' says Sam. 'So it *is* a hacking job?'

'Not quite,' Kat corrects him. 'City Hall has an Internet firewall big as a festival perimeter. Nobody can get through it, over it or under it.' She pauses there to make sure everyone has understood her right. 'Guys, the only way is by gaining access to the building and taking a look at his computer for ourselves.'

'You mean *break in*?' Jude isn't alone in being taken aback by the plan. Even Tiny Ti rolls her eyes. 'City Hall is crawling with security staff!' he continues. 'Trust me, I know. My mum works there, and she can't get into the building without bag checks, ID passes and all sorts.'

'Maybe she could have a look for us,' Marvin suggests, and falls quiet when he realises that would be out of the question. 'OK, so how else are we gonna do it? The Marshal works at the very top of one of the tallest buildings in the city. You can't even see the dome from ground level, which means someone's gonna have to head up there to find out what's really cookin'.'

Kat shrugs. 'It's all we can do,' she tells them. 'If we don't give it a go this could be our final weekend in the wasteland.'

The crew consider this in silence. 'I guess that means we might as well make the most of our last Saturday here,' says Tiny Ti, clutching her board like a baby doll now. 'Ain't nothing going to save us now but a superhero.'

Without another word, she breaks for the half pipe and drops out of sight. It's clear she's feeling sad, but determined not to let it get the better of her. Marvin isn't far behind, nor Spinner, Crash, Kat and even Sam. All of them follow her lead, and start leaping and looping from one lip to the other like balls in a tombola. And that's how they celebrate the last hour of light, each of them whooping with every trick as the fire goes out of the sky and the stars begin to blink. Only one of their number sits it out, too scared to join in, in case he goes aerial and stays there once again.

The last thing Jude wants now is for Kat to think he can pull off the impossible.

Plan ahead two moves at a time. That was what Benjamin Three-Sixty had told him. The problem is where to begin. Not only is there City Hall to consider, but also the small matter of asking out the girl who could reduce him to jelly just by looking at him. It's a weak point that doesn't exactly mark him out as a superhero in the making, he thinks to himself – just a loser like his dad.

six

There was no need to call upon the services of a superhero to access the Marshal's computer. That's what Spinner had advised the crew, and Spinner regarded himself as resident expert on these matters. A visit to his bedroom could back him up. The place was stacked with so many comics you could barely see the walls. From Superman to The Silver Surfer, the Hulk and back again, Spinner had collected them all, and claimed to know everything there was to know about such defenders of humanity.

'For a start they don't exist,' he told them bluntly. 'People used to think they were real many years ago, but the world is all grown up now. Nobody can get away with wearing their pants on the outside without being laughed at, and a mask just marks you out as a bank robber. Anyway, who needs stretchy limbs or fly-like suckers on their hands when all you gotta do is walk in the front door with a lot of charm and bags of confidence?'

Which was how Spinner came to insist that *he* should be the one to enter City Hall first thing Monday morning. By the time they made it on to school, he had promised, they could relax through lessons safe in the knowledge that the wasteland would be there for them when the final bell rang out.

'That boy is one jump short of a skate park. He's never gonna make it.' Marvin shakes his head and eases back on to his stool. The crew are in the sushi bar on the opposite side of the street. Jude sits between Kat and Tiny Ti. He pays no attention to the conveyor belt currently parading all kinds of fish delicacies between the crew and the window. Like everyone else, his focus is fixed on the double doors over there. City Hall is a building as impressive as it is imposing: a mix of gothic stonework, Greek-style pillars and modern, mirrored windows that rise up towards the sky. In keeping with the neighbouring buildings, it towers so high you can't even see the crowning glass dome from where Marshal Dawe is said to keep watch. Every block was the same as this one, forming not so much a busy urban thoroughfare but a canyon made from steel and bricks and endless windows. The kind that only saw the sun when it sailed over the strip of sky overhead.

'I know I said this was the only way,' Kat mutters bitterly. 'But I was thinking perhaps we could've come up with something a little more foolproof.'

Jude catches her eyes when she says this, and quickly looks away. Was she suggesting that he should've been the one who found another way in? Already he's beginning to feel like this is a personal test he's failing fast. He glances at his watch. Any time now, his mum could turn up for work having dropped off Sam at junior school. If she spots him in here, when he's supposed to be in the yard waiting for first bell, he knows for sure she'll come right in and make a scene.

'I think we should at least give Spin a chance,' Jude says instead, though he doesn't sound convincing. Even Crash seems concerned. He's seated at the far end, beside the stool reserved for his absent friend, nervously tapping his chopsticks on the edge of the food bar. For the city's biggest sushi fan, his loss of appetite speaks volumes.

Two minutes earlier, Spinner had swaggered up the steps to the lobby, dressed up like a pizza delivery boy. He had the red baseball cap with the logo on the front, the matching polo shirt, the shorts, the whole works. He was even carrying a Pepperoni Hot in a cardboard tray – both the outfit and the deep pan being a favour from a friend who had a part-time job at a takeaway joint. What he planned to do was waltz in with an order that had come from the Marshal's office, and use his wits to take him all the way to the top. *People in an office get hungry*, he had assured them, the last thing he said, in fact, before leaving them to watch from the sushi bar. *Nobody's going to phone upstairs to check. Pizza gets delivered here all the time.*

It is only now, some minutes after Spinner made his move on City Hall, that Marvin identifies a flaw in the plan.

'It's just gone quarter to nine,' he says. 'Who eats pizza at this time in the morning?'

'Who eats *sushi* this time in the morning?' Tiny Ti pulls a face at a dish of raw cod slices gliding by on the conveyor belt. 'Even Crash can't face it today.'

Crash doesn't appear to hear, however. He's still tapping out that edgy beat, just watching and waiting. Whatever's going on behind the lobby glass over there, it's clear he doesn't like it. Not one little bit.

'Has anyone thought what might go down if Dawe happens to be at his desk?' Now it's Jude's turn to cast doubt on this mission. 'Then again, if anyone can sweet talk his way out of a sticky situation, it's Spinner.'

'Just don't ask me to go in there and get him,' says Marvin. 'I know I'm big for my age, but security staff are always bigger.'

'Someone has to do it,' says his little cousin, prompting Jude to eye his skateboard. There it is, propped up against the window, standing sentry like all the others but looking like it's seen the most action. He's had this deck since he first found his feet: the scuffed stickers plastered over it like a personal diary only he can read. For Jude, this board is an extension of his body. He can move on it without even thinking, sometimes, in the same way that you walk, sprint or leap.

But then, at a time like this, it's better to leave the board alone and use your head instead.

Jude sits upright again, finds the whole crew waiting for him to say something. 'If he's not out in five minutes,' he says, after sighing long and hard, 'I'll walk in and explain that we're just kids fooling around with a bad dare gone wrong. If security get heavy I can always call upon my mum to save us.'

Kat says: 'You make her sound like *she's* the one with special powers,' but it's clear to Jude from the way she grins that he's just done the right thing. This time he relishes her smile, only for the moment to be overtaken by Crash who suddenly leaps to his feet. They wheel around to see him looking both alarmed and overjoyed, and immediately follow his line of sight across the street.

'Speaking of special powers,' says Marvin dryly, just as the lobby doors snap open, 'it looks to me like Spinner's discovered he can fly.'

Fortunately, Spin is still clutching the pizza box. It saves him from serious injury as he comes in to land at the top of the steps, even if it does leave him with a face full of tomato and mozzarella. Behind him, the two large men in uniform who have just ejected him from the building dust off their hands and leave him to pick himself up. People stop, stare, but mostly laugh and go about their business. All except one woman, who appears to recognise him.

'Oi, Jude!' Now Tiny Ti is up on her feet, even if it does make it hard for her to see over the conveyor belt. 'Isn't that your mum?'

'Nah,' jokes Marvin. 'Jude's mum has a beard.'

'Yeah, yeah.' Jude collects his board as he stops him there, careful not to be seen from the street.

'A beard and a big bar code tattooed across the back of her neck. It ain't pretty, people.'

'Enough with the mum cusses, huh? There's a time and a place for everything. Besides,' Jude adds, unable to resist a comeback of his own, 'your mum's so big she has time zones of her own.'

The insults continue as the crew prepare to move out of the sushi bar. Even Tiny Ti joins in, but nobody actually means it. All of them know it's just a cheap and easy way to raise a smile, and avoid a grim reality. For with no access to the Marshal's computer, the wasteland is as good as lost.

seven

The man considers the question with his back to the kid from the newspaper. He doesn't turn or even glance at this junior reporter with the side-scraped hair, the starter suit and the camera slung round his neck. All the man does is sit there in that leather swivel chair, contemplating the view through the glass. It's so high up here you can't even hear the traffic in the boulevards below. Not a single car horn or siren. Some of the neighbouring scrapers dare to climb higher, as if to grab some of the unbroken sunlight and cleaner air that contributes to this sense of absolute peace. That doesn't bother him too bad, though, because the owners paid a sky-high tax for the privilege, plus 'expenses'. Besides, the building he's in takes centre stage, like an all-seeing eye. For this isn't just any view that the figure behind the desk is facing, but one from the top of City Hall's fabled glass dome.

The kid from the newspaper is awestruck. He's barely blinked since arriving, and not just because he's one of the few citizens to have actually seen the inside of this panoramic penthouse with his own eyes. For a moment, he dares to look up and around. The glass panelling right over his head is so seamless that it feels like he's in some kind of suicidal open-top office. His head goes giddy at the very idea, forcing him to grip the edge of his chair. He reminds himself that they're completely sealed in, but that just makes him think of upturned fishbowls, even killing jars. Either way, he's desperate to recover his head for heights and be as cool as he can.

As you couldn't actually see the dome from ground level, tall stories and urban myths continually sprang up around both the structure itself and the man he's here to interview. That he has yet to turn around and face him directly, does nothing for the kid's nerves. It's his first time out as a reporter, too. Strictly speaking, he's the paper's work experience boy: offering his services after school to operate the photocopier or fetch coffee. Then City Hall call up the news desk and invite someone to profile the man in charge: a chance for the next generation of voters to get inside the mind of the Marshal. Suddenly all eyes fall on him. The kid couldn't believe it at the time, and he's still finding it hard to take in. Talk about trial by fire.

'Take your time, sir,' he says, unable to stand the silence. 'If you want, we can move on to another question.'

All he can see of Marshal J Dawe is the top of his ten-gallon hat, and the smoke from his cigar that keeps rising like so many thought balloons. Trouble is the kid can't read anything in them. All he knows is that he began by asking Dawe to comment on the East/West divide within the city, in particular the tensions it had created among the young people, and *this* was how he responded. The kid glances at his notebook, wishing he could write something in it, and catches his breath as the Marshal finally speaks.

'May I ask where you live?'

'East side,' he replies, sensing somehow that this is the wrong answer, more so when he sees Dawe nodding to himself. 'We almost moved West, but times got tough for my folks, and, well, y'know how it is.'

His words trail away, and that's when the Marshal spins round in his chair. All the kid can think is how different he looks in the flesh. On the television and in the papers he's always flashing a big grin. It didn't matter if he was answering difficult questions – Dawe never let go of the look that won elections. Which is why it comes as quite a shock to see him now. With his lips flattened together in what could be a look of annoyance or irritation, it's his eyes that command all the attention. They're hard as marble, and way too pale and penetrating under the brim of that stupid hat. Perhaps Marshal Dawe picks up on this from the kid's startled expression, because those pearly white teeth emerge just then and spread into a smile. 'Before I can comment on your question,' he says, tipping back his hat with his forefinger, 'I should like to invite you on a tour of the West to see "how it is" for yourself. I'm keen for you to meet some of the boys from the community over there, because you'll find they're hard-working, decent members of this city as a whole. None of them understand why these vandals from the East feel the need to pursue a turf war, and I believe you can set the record straight in your article. What do you say?'

The kid has barely registered the offer before the phone starts ringing. Marshal J Dawe grabs the receiver without once taking his eyes off this snot-nosed idiot the paper has dispatched. It's a pain having him here, but then it is just what he'd ordered. It would make his own job much easier, after all: selling the story he has planned.

The kid swallows hard, wishing he'd been assigned to a desk job, and watches the Marshal's smile begin to tighten and shrink.

'Young man,' says Dawe, masking the mouthpiece with his palm, 'did you order a pizza delivery?'

'Me?' he squeaks, shaking his head already. 'I'm here for an interview, that's all.'

Dawe refuses to let him look away, as if searching his face for a sign that this is some kind of prank, then turns to the third person in the room: a youth with a long face, a leather trench coat and dirty blond hair that hangs over his upturned collar. He's been slouched on a sofa in the far corner all this time, a pair of rollerblades in his lap. The kid figures they've seen some action, judging by the odour of sweaty feet that taints the air. When the Marshal enquires if the pizza order is his doing, this idle-looking blader stops toying with the wheels and raises his hands to express his innocence.

'Not me, Pop, but I can always use a deep pan if that's what's on offer. We can eat it in the limo. Is it seafood?'

The Marshal begins to relay the question down the line, then cuts himself off when he realises what he's doing. He slams the receiver back and climbs to his feet, but just as it looks as if he's about to kick off at his son that trademark grin reappears.

'You'll excuse my boy, won't you? He likes to be the funny guy sometimes, but he's a good lad and I think you'll find his friends are, too. Now, come with us, we're going for a little ride.'

'What?' The kid hangs back. 'I . . . I can't. I have school first. I assumed this would just be a short interview.'

The Marshal and his son glance at one another. Although neither shows a trace of emotion, the kid can sense some tension building under the glass.

'You're right,' says Dawe, and chuckles to himself. Then he turns to address his son directly. 'You don't want to miss out on your studies either, *do you*?'

The youth tries hard not to look like he's sucking on a particularly bitter wedge of lemon, but agrees that's just what he was going to point out, too. 'Education is where it's at, Pop.'

'Indeed,' the Marshal agrees. 'Let's take Scoop out after last bell instead. Meet us outside City Hall,' he suggests, 'and bring your camera.'

The kid from the newspaper? He doesn't know what to make of all this. His editor had told him to just be polite at all times, and there's no way he'd find the nerve to decline this exclusive offer. As Marshal J Dawe escorts him to the dome's spiral stairwell, he can't help fretting about this guided tour they've lined up after school. Even with the cushioned suspension of a luxury limousine, all the vibes he's getting suggest it's going to be one heck of a bumpy ride.

eight

The rest of Jude's school day seemed to move like syrup. From double Ecology in the morning, right through Urban Economics last thing that afternoon, all he could do was watch the clock hands struggle towards last bell. Not that there was anything to be done when the moment finally arrived. The crew had already sent in their spy to see what the Marshal was cooking with the wasteland, and look what happened there.

'If anyone else calls me pizza face, I swear they'll be seeing stars long before night falls.' Spinner speaks like he means business, rolling slowly home through the alleyways with Crash, Marvin and Jude. He's scrubbed up as best he can, but you can still see tomato paste in his hairline. The polite thing would've been to ignore it. Then again, Spin also reeks of mixed herbs, and that doesn't happen every day.

'OK, we'll go easy from now on.' Marvin leads the way down the shadow-strewn shortcut between one block and the next. 'Although it does serve you right for thinking you could ever measure up carrying the full twelve inches.' He brings his own board to a halt, just at the mouth of the alley, causing everyone to narrowly avoid piling up behind him.

When the boys recover, they look up to find Marvin filling the space ahead with a great big idiot grin. He may be talking about the diameter of the pizza that Spin had chosen, but everyone knows he means something completely different – and a whole lot more personal, too.

'You gotta be more realistic when it comes to size,' he continues now, and shows everyone the gap between his thumb and forefinger. 'Something smaller would've looked more natural on a guy like you.'

Spinner has to wait for the boys to pull themselves together before he can speak. By the time their laughter fades, he has squared right up to the big guy. 'You trying to say something, doughballs?' He jabs a finger into Marvin's jelly belly, unwilling to step down now his manhood's been called into question. 'You may be larger than life, pal, but I got a whole lot more to offer where it really counts.' Spinner finishes there, and shakes out one track-suited leg as if to create more room inside.

Without a word, Marvin comes across like a wave on the point of crashing. He rises to his full height, blocking out the street scene behind him, and casts the darkest shadow of all over this boy who dares to diss him. 'You're a mate,' he growls. 'Which means it's only right I give you the chance to apologise.'

Spinner shrinks from his presence, only to connect with Crash, who in turn stumbles backwards into the one boy here who's keen to keep things in perspective.

'Fellas,' says Jude. 'Can we please stop grabbing our crotches and focus on the only big issue that matters?'

It's here that Spinner and Marvin appear to find common ground. They glance at each other, then at Crash, before Spin comes back and says: 'What else is more important than dick size?'

'It's your *brain* size you should be worried about,' Jude tells him. 'What about the wasteland?'

'What about it?' Marvin seems genuinely mystified. 'We tried our best, and look what happened. It's over, Jude. Time to face facts.' He pauses there for a moment, and Jude just knows that the sudden gleam in his eye means the spotlight is about to switch. 'Anyway, why are *you* so keen to avoid the subject? Does the truth hurt?' The big guy wiggles his little finger to demonstrate what he's talking about, much to Jude's unease.

'Everything's fine in that department,' he says, weakly, thinking at the same time that he's no idea what's normal. How could he? It wasn't the kind of thing you compared and contrasted, after all.

'Are you sure there's no room for improvement?' asks Marvin, addressing everyone again.

'Whatever!' Jude crosses his arms defensively, and waits

in vain for the lads to accept his word for it. 'Will you stop looking like you don't believe me?' he says finally. 'It's none of your business, anyways.'

Nudging Crash in the ribs, Spinner says, 'Jude's just a bit uptight 'cos he's so-in-love-with-Kat.'

Crash stifles a smirk as his mate sets this line to song, which only serves to encourage the boys to make life even harder for Jude. They don't mean anything by it, even Jude knows that. He just has to take it on the chin. Ragging one another like this was almost a team sport – something the lads did together when the girls weren't around – and if you didn't get in first the attention would only turn to you. Another time, it could be Spinner, Crash or Marvin in the firing line and Jude would be giving as good as he is getting right now. Perhaps his unease is evident, because Marvin calls a halt to the mickey-taking and agrees they should keep moving.

'Save it till we get back,' he says, climbing back on to his board. 'We all know it isn't safe to stand around outside our turf. Not with the West Crew looking for some payback.' He pushes out of the alleyway, but Spinner and Crash stay where they are, and appear to consult each other without speaking.

'It's sushi time for me and my man,' Spin declares.

'It's *always* sushi time for you two,' says Jude. 'Don't you think of anything but your stomachs?'

'Sushi is a way of life,' Spinner tells him. 'Can't skate or spray without some good soul food inside us. We'll catch you later.'

The pair break south on their boards, weaving around pedestrians as they sniff out any place that serves their favourite food. Marvin shrugs and moves eastwards, rolling home now with Jude at his side.

'So,' he says, as the wheels rumble over the pavement. 'What are you gonna do about it?'

'About what?'

'You know.'

Jude doesn't need to ask if he's talking about Kat. It's clear from the way Marvin raises the issue without a side-glance or sneer that he's giving him a break now – a chance for Jude to talk freely without risk of being ridiculed.

'I want to ask her out,' he says after a moment. 'But I'm worried about how she'll react. Benjamin Three-Sixty reckons I need to think two steps ahead and stick to it.'

'The old DJ with his head in the clouds? He's probably right, though. You can't put a foot wrong up there on his roof, else you'll take a tumble.'

Jude smiles, says: 'If Kat knocks me back, it will be the worst crash and burn I've ever experienced.'

'D'you think that's likely?'

'Things will never be the same again if she says no.'

'Things ain't gonna be the same again if she says *yes*.' Now he shares a look with Jude. A glint in his eye with a grin underneath it. 'Bet you're thinking how much easier life would be if she asked *you* out.'

They wheel across a junction, pushing wide around an elderly woman with a blue rinse hairdo and a mean-looking pit bull on a chain. An odd combination, but wise for someone her age.

'Do you think she might?' asks Jude.

'Nope. Not a chance in hell.'

Jude pulls up as they reach the pavement, waits for Marvin to stop and faces him directly. 'You're not exactly filling me with confidence, here. Do you know something?'

'All I know is Kat's crazy about you, but she isn't the kind of girl who's going to make the first move. That would mean dropping her guard, and letting everyone know she's just as vulnerable on the inside as the rest of us.'

Jude digests this with a long sigh. 'She isn't making it very easy for me.'

'Which makes it all the more rewarding if you get a result,' says Marvin. 'But you gotta get in there before someone else does. Seize the moment, Jude. Be the man.'

The pair push on, mindful not to cut round blind corners just in case they come face to face with the bladers from the West. It isn't a big deal for the boys. Growing up in the city, this kind of precaution is second nature. What concerns

Jude right now are the three tower blocks that have just swung into view.

'OK, there's no time like the present. I'm going to call round and ask her. How do I look?'

Marvin gives him the once-over. 'Shiny,' he says, 'but good.'

'Shiny?'

'Your face, mate. I can almost see myself in it.'

Jude senses himself deflate. He drops off his board, kicks it into his grip, and trudges on beside his friend. The thing with his skin is like all the other surprises going off inside him right now. Not just the hairy bits and the niffy pits, but the strength of his feelings for a girl, even his relationship with the board beneath his feet – and yet for all he knew this could be standard issue for Marvin and any other boy his age. The problem was nobody dared speak up in case they wound up being labelled a freak. Then again, thinks Jude, if any friend was going to understand how it felt to be different, his great big buddy beside him would be the one. He takes a deep breath, hopes like hell this won't be held against him, and says: 'Can I ask you something personal?'

'Try me,' says Marvin.

'When you look in the mirror nowadays,' he continues hesitantly, 'what do you see?'

'You mean which bit? If I want to see my whole self, I

gotta step back a long way so it fits in the frame, and my bedroom ain't big enough for that.'

'I'm serious,' says Jude. 'Lately, I look at my reflection and I barely recognise myself.'

'You're growing up. We all are. It's a fact of life.'

'I know, but some things take my breath away.'

'Yeah? Please don't say this is building up to a knob gag. I thought we left that back in the alley with Spinner and Crash.'

Jude laughs and tells him that isn't what he had in mind. 'Marv, even *I* know there's some stuff guys keep to themselves.'

'Exactly,' he agrees. 'Never put your pecker up for proper discussion. Boast about it by all means, but I really don't want to know what's going on down there, just as I don't want *you* to know what's going on with *mine*. You ever have a problem? Take it to the doctor, that's if you have the balls.'

They come to a halt by a bench, where the street opens up into a sprawling concrete island surrounding the three blocks. A scattering of cars could be seen in the spaces provided, but most people from The Projects moved around by overhead rail, or subway. A vehicle was a target for robbers and vandals, as all the busted glass made plain. Just looking around, they see clusters of it glinting in the afternoon sun like diamonds dropped in a heist. Marvin glances over his shoulder, not just scoping for bladers but for anyone who might overhear them. Then he looks directly at the Laundromat opposite, the one with the grilled windows and the weeds growing from the roof, and says, 'What's on your mind, Jude?'

'That's exactly what I'm finding hard to deal with. I feel wired, Marv, like a power switch has been thrown inside my brain, one that's primed me for something but I don't know what.'

Marvin shrugs. 'Too much caffeine?'

'I don't drink coffee. Besides, it's a bigger buzz than that. It makes me think too much about things.'

'Like?'

'Like *everything*. Who I am, where I've come from and what's in store as I get older. I look at Mum and feel there's so much more I could be doing to help her, I look at Sam and think he'll grow up to be as confused as me, and I don't even know where to *start* with Kat. A couple of years ago, I would've hit on her without worrying about it.'

'A couple of years ago,' Marvin reminds Jude, 'you wouldn't have *noticed* Kat, not in that way. Buddy, it's just a phase we're all going through.'

'But I really feel it's building up to something,' Jude insists. 'This buzz has been in my head for ages now, but it's starting to get physical . . . ' He tails off there, thinking that perhaps it isn't such a good idea to pick apart the electric moment that happened in the half pipe because it really was too way out for words.

'It's your hormones,' Marvin concludes suddenly – a bid to reassure him. 'They mess up your mind, your body, your *life*, it sometimes seems.'

'You make it sound like you've been there, done that, bought the T-shirt to prove it.'

'Not really,' Marvin says, settling on the bench now. He spreads his arms along the back of it, as if taking Jude under his wing. 'I got growing pains like you wouldn't believe.'

'That's no surprise, a guy your size.'

'I sweat for no reason, and mostly each mornings I wake up and pray I haven't made a sticky mess of the sheets. Nowadays I daren't look my mum in the face when she does the laundry.' Marvin glances at Jude, baffled as to why he's just inched nervously towards the end of the bench. Then he thinks back a beat, and offers him a skewed and goofy smile. 'Too much information?'

'Damn right,' says Jude, laughing now. 'That kind of careless talk is out of bounds. You really ought to practise what you preach.'

'I do what I can,' chuckles the big guy. 'Sometimes, though, you gotta get things off your chest, you know?'

The pair turn to the boards at their feet, as if that's a safe place to look.

'If my dad was around,' says Jude eventually, 'I guess I'd be talking to him about stuff like this. You can do that kind of thing with dads.'

'Maybe so.' Marvin nods, but doesn't sound entirely convinced.

'If things were different, mine would have been sober enough to offer good advice.'

'All families have their problems,' Marvin tells him, looking up and around. The sun is still shining on this late afternoon but the light is strangely weak. 'We just do the best we can,' he concludes, 'and turn to friends when times get tough.'

Jude smiles to himself. 'You talk a lot of sense sometimes.'

'Sure I do,' says Marvin, chuckling, 'for a *kid*! I may look older, but I'm only about to turn fourteen, same as you. That's why you don't want someone like me around when you make your move on Kat. 'Case you say something dumb and I'm obliged to make your life a misery.' Marvin hoists his frame off the bench, hitching his big pants straight around his waist as he does so. 'You should listen to Benjamin. Whenever I tune in he's always spinning crazy tunes, but the guy still talks sense in between.' He stops there, licks his finger and tests the breeze. 'It's time I split,' he says. 'I'll catch you later.'

'Don't you fancy a skate first? We've maybe got a day before the bulldozers move in.'

'Nah,' says Marvin, and collects his deck. 'We gave it a proper good send-off at the weekend. Besides, you know I don't like getting my hair wet.'

'But it isn't raining!'

The big guy swings his chin to the East, inviting Jude to look in the same direction. Dusk always kicks in first over there, but it's a little too early for that just yet. Even so, the horizon line is unnaturally dark and appears to be thickening. When a storm came in over the wasteland, it always had plenty of time and space to mass into a very powerful force indeed.

Marvin comes back round again, taps his nose like he's in possession of some kind of insider information. 'Trust me, Jude, something's gonna break over this city real soon.'

nine

The kid from the newspaper has never been this far West in his entire life. He wouldn't *dream* of venturing out here on his own, though he has to admit the wide streets and all the boutiques beat the boarded-up shop-fronts he's grown so used to.

'In an ideal world,' he says, 'the whole city would look like this.'

He's in the back of the limo, sandwiched between the Marshal and his son, which at least stops him sliding to and fro on the leather seats each time the chauffeur takes a corner. It also stops him getting out, should things get too uncomfortable. Marshal Dawe says nothing in response to his comment. He just nods and smiles, lets the kid find his own answer, but never turns his attention away from the passenger window. His son, meantime, hasn't taken his eyes off their guest since they pulled away from City Hall. He's right there on his opposite side, those rollerblades now laced up on his feet and a knowing look all over his face. Weird. More so since Dawe still hasn't actually introduced him. He doesn't even know his name.

'So, how was college today?' this fledgling reporter asks. It's all he knows about him, but at least it breaks the ice. 'My tutor couldn't believe it when I told him you guys were taking me on a tour after last lesson.'

'Huh?' The son looks mystified, but something seems to click once he glances across at his father. 'Oh, *college*! Yeah! 'Course I was there. Where else would I be? I'm majoring in law right now, but I hope one day to follow my father into politics.'

'Oh, really?' At last, he has something to write in his notebook, even if it did sound a little bit forced.

'Pop is a hero, in my book. Some of the things he's done for this city are just amazing. Take this new recycling plant he's landed for the East. At the moment the site is just a grubby wasteland, a magnet for vandals, addicts and delinquents with no respect for the law. This venture guarantees a change for the better over there, you mark my words.'

The kid from the paper glances up from his notes, only to be greeted by an encouraging gesture from the guy to write it down in full. *Jeez! Was 'mouth piece' one or two words?* Still, he has no choice but to tell it like they say it, just as his editor has briefed him. One day he'll get a scoop, maybe in a couple of years, but for now those investigative tendencies just can't come out to play. There is no way he can head back to the news desk on his first day in the field with a story about a Marshal who smells this fishy. If he did, most probably the powers that be in City Hall would go nuts with the paper and he'd be squashed from a great height. It would end his career before he had even left school, and he's wanted this for so long. 'One thing,' he says, still scrawling words across the page. 'If I'm going to quote this, I really need to know your name.'

'His name is Jack,' says the Marshal, as if the boy can't be trusted to speak for himself. 'Jack Dawe, after me – but we call him Jack Junior, so he has something to aspire to. It's never too early to encourage ambition, I feel.'

'That's cool,' says the kid from the newspaper, thinking at the same time: *Jack Dawe? What kind of parents name their child after a bird with a thief's eye? Worse still, what kind of child would grow up to pass on that burden to his own son?* The kid from the newspaper has just underscored the name when he senses the limo turn and slow. He looks up once more, just as the chauffeur draws to a halt at the wrought iron entrance to a cemetery. It's the size of a street square, and surrounded by mansions, but could be a jungle inside.

'Here we are.' Marshal Dawe climbs out of the vehicle, the spurs on his boots clicking against the tarmac. 'Follow me, Scoop.'

He does as he's told, aware that Jack Junior is right on his tail because he can hear his rollerblades travelling over the cracked and blistered path. The cemetery is a little run-down, but nowhere near as bad as the standard of neglect you'd find back East. There's no overcrowding here, either, just block after block of elaborate mausoleums and monuments to the dead, shaded by lime trees and rhododendron bushes. It's like a city within a city, fringed as it is by the roofs of all these plush houses, but he doesn't even want to think about the citizens hemmed in here. Instead, he struggles to keep up with the Marshal, and wonders if that rumbling sound behind him could be any closer. It doesn't help that the air feels locked and loaded on this day: primed for some kind of strike. He glances up, finds the sky suspiciously clear. Wherever he's being taken now, he'd like to be somewhere safe and sound should the weather turn against them.

'Can I ask what we're here to see?' the reporter dares to say next, upon which the Marshal spins on his boot heels to face him, palms spread like he only has to use his eyes.

'Just look around,' he replies, without stopping, and that's when the kid from the newspaper swears he hears another set of wheels swoop by. He glances over his shoulder, sees some movement behind a gargoyle. Then he looks back, and finds a horseshoe of rollerbladers have gathered on the path right in front of the Marshal. *Oh no*, he thinks, *it's an ambush!* A cry dies in his throat, and he jumps when Jack Junior glides past him. The Marshal watches his son join his fellow bladers up ahead. As ever, he's beaming away. There's no way the kid can be sure what's behind it, and that chills him to the bone.

'Here are the people I wanted you to meet,' he says, and fires up a cigar. 'Last week, this cemetery was littered with all kinds of garbage, but these fine boys cleaned it up.' He steps aside, invites the kid to take a good look. 'We're talking about the faces of this city's future, young man. They volunteered to pick up the cigarette cartons and the empty cans, gathering together the first shipment for the new recycling plant.'

He's walking again as he talks, leading the young reporter between this sullen gang, to a clearing just behind them. Sure enough, there's a skip filled with all kinds of refuse, including a rusted cooker. As the plant has yet to be constructed, it's kind of a token gesture, but the kid from the newspaper is smart enough not to raise the issue. Instead, he plucks the notebook from his inside pocket, and dutifully scratches out another line – anything to stop the Marshal's smile from disappearing off his face again. He's only witnessed a glimpse of the real man behind that mask, but he really doesn't fancy seeing it again.

'My boy organised this clear-up campaign because he couldn't stand to see the place turn into the same kind of state as that wasteland. He enrolled his friends to help him, too, and do you know what? Every single one offered their time without question. If only those graffiti-crazed kids from the East followed their example, this city would be a better place.'

'Right,' says the kid, unable to picture this mob dedicating their time to such a fine example of good citizenship. The fact that most glance away when he meets their eyes tells him a lot more than anything the Marshal has to say, but still he nods and pretends to be impressed. The kid even knows some of the graffiti artists round his way. A few skate on the wasteland out behind the project block where he lives, and they've always struck him as decent people. Whatever you thought of graffiti, it had to be better than just getting off your face because there was nothing else to do. Still, he records the Marshal's account, hoping that perhaps he can talk it down a little when it comes to writing it up. *Some day*, he thinks, *I'm going to be in a position to uncover the story behind this story. Then you'll be sorry you invited me here to do your dirty work.* He punches a full stop on to the page and flips shut his notebook. 'Thanks, guys,' he says through gritted teeth. 'This is all really interesting.'

'Our pleasure, Scoop. Now why don't you take a pretty picture of these fine boys so they can make their mums proud when they read tomorrow's paper?'

'Sure thing. I almost forgot.'

The kid shoots off half a roll of film, figuring that at

least a picture of these shifty-looking youths will say more than the finished article. As soon as he's through, he feels the Marshal's meaty paw on his shoulder, guiding him around. All the way back up the cemetery path he's puffing on his cigar and talking about how much he's looking forward to reading the piece when it appears in the paper, but this cub reporter can't help but listen to the muttered cross-talk going on behind him.

'*Man, that was easy. What a schmuck! Thanks, fellas.*'

'*No worries, so long as we get paid like you promised.*'

'*Relax. Pa's got it all sorted. Soon as the recycling plant starts doing business, I'll be the one who cleans up, I swear.*'

'*You'd better be, Jack Junior. Else there'll be trouble.*'

All the kid wants to do is turn around and listen, but the Marshal's hand stays firm, and leaves him no choice but to keep up the pace.

'Scoop, you're a credit to the East side. With your help I really feel we can improve the less attractive aspects of your neighbourhood. Mark my words, it'll come up smelling of roses in no time – just like this place.'

The kid is encouraged to look around, and he has to admit it's a peaceful kind of place to be. Perhaps that's what has drawn the figure up ahead, he thinks: the one who lurches without warning from behind a marble pillar supporting one of the mausoleums. He doesn't look like he's in a good way, almost staggering before finding his balance. The man is wearing a full-length duffle coat, stained by who knows what, and trousers that are plainly too big for him. He's also muttering to himself at random, and it's clear he's in a world of his own. The kid also notices he's clutching something in his hand, wrapped up in brown paper. A bottle it seems, when he pauses to swig from the mouth of it, before swaying on his way. Just then the young reporter senses the hand on his shoulder grow heavy, slowing him to a stop.

'Hey, punk!' This is the Marshal, who leaves the kid standing now. 'Hobos like you don't belong around here! Scram back to your own side of the city before I call the cops!'

The man peers over his shoulder, looking both surprised and annoyed, and immediately the Marshal stops dead in his tracks. Unlike Dawe, he looks battered in all kinds of ways: his face is a contrast of coal-dark stubble and leathery skin, but his eyes burn so bright he could be years younger than his weathered appearance suggests. A powerful silence falls between the two men, and the kid wonders if the guy has any idea who he's staring out here. To his surprise, however, it's the Marshal who breaks away first – but not before crushing the smouldering stub of his stogie beneath one boot heel.

'C'mon, Scoop,' he says, striding back now, 'let's take another path. A drunk like that is a danger to himself and other people, and as you're in my charge this afternoon I have to make your safety a priority.'

'Sure thing, sir. I agree he doesn't look like the kind of crazy you'd want to mess with.'

The kid glances back to see the drunk moving the other way. When he looks back at the Marshal, he finds his face burned up with anger, and thinks better of chasing him up on his policy towards the city's drifters. The way those eyes of his are fixed on the exit ahead, he figures it might be wise to pretend the incident never happened at all.

ten

This is the plan: first Jude will head home for a long hot soak in the tub. Once he's towelled himself dry, he'll lose himself in a mist of anti-perspirant spray and rehearse his opening lines a few times in the mirror. After that, he'll dig out his favourite hoodie and a pair of combats, maybe snap on his fly-like wraparound shades. Once he's happy with his appearance, he'll head up a few flights and knock on Kat's door. Naturally, he'll be super nice to her stepmother, even though she doesn't speak any English (which means a bright smile is essential, so he'll have to brush his teeth, too) and, finally, when he's alone with the girl who has come to form the axis of his world, he'll take a deep breath and ask her directly for that date he's been building up to for so long now. Whatever happens, at least he'll have got it out of his system, and hopefully he'll be able to feel some sense of normality again.

Two steps. That was how Benjamin Three-Sixty had insisted that he make his move. Everything seems to fall into place as Jude makes his way towards his block. All it has taken is a pep talk from his friend plus a little space to himself, and suddenly it seems like the only way forward. It would be just like attempting the kind of insane skate trick that either ended in death or glory. You didn't head down a suicide slope without first getting into the right state of mind, and when it came to this bid for a date that started with looking your best. With no worries about bad breath or big hair, you were free to concentrate and commit. No change of heart. No turning back. No fear.

It feels good now he knows exactly how to handle things. Benjamin was right, he thinks. Marvin, too. He's waiting for the elevator at the foot of his block, trying hard not to breathe in the stink from the bin bags piled up in the pen behind him. He takes a step away, and finds his reflection in the elevator's brushed steel door. It's hard to see much, just a blur in between spaghetti-like loops of graffiti. Still, he reflects, that's probably no bad thing.

Given what he knows about his current complexion, Kat would probably find him as appealing as the stink from the bins. His confidence would only take a knock if he saw his greasy mug before he'd had a chance to scrub up. It would be like racing towards a ramp, and spotting a stone in your tracks . . . or surfacing from your thoughts, as Jude does when the lift doors finally part, to find yourself face to face with the one girl you *really* don't want to see you in this state.

'Hey!'

'Hi Jude.' She barely seems to register him, standing as she is with her nose buried in a clutch of documents.

'Wha— why . . . I mean, how're you doing?'

Marking her place with one long finger, Katya steps out, cool as shade. 'Good,' she says absently, and finally quits looking at the papers in her hand. 'OK, not great,' she admits. She loops her hair behind one ear, bangles jangling, as she catches his eye and smiles. Jude turns his attention to the papers, still reeling at her presence. It looks like she's studying technical drawings: some cross-section of rooms, corridors and stairwells.

'City Hall?' he asks, struggling not to fall apart on her now.

'What else?' She fans through the drawings so he can see for himself. 'I found it on the architect's homepage, printed it off during lunch break, but I wish I hadn't. We already know the place is like a fortress, and this just proves it. Only way in is from the top down, like that's going to happen.'

Kat returns her attention to Jude, but he's barely taken in a word she just said. A minute earlier he'd been rehearsing how to ask her out. Now here she is, catching him unprepared, and his mind has gone completely blank. When he braves looking at her again, he finds she's tipped her head to one side as if trying to get another angle on him.

'Are we OK?' she asks, smiling quizzically.

'*We?*' he says, without thinking. 'D'you mean us, or me?'

'I mean *you*, dipstick. It's a figure of speech. A term of affection.'

This isn't part of the plan, he thinks, but what choice does he have now she's come out of the elevator using words like *we* and *affection*! It means skipping step one for step two if he's going to seize the moment, but with no time to prepare or psyche himself up. *This is all too much*, he thinks to himself. *It's now or never*.

'Kat,' he says, but it comes out as a squeak, dammit. Already his cheeks have turned an angry crimson, and panic begins to kick in. He feels like crying. A lump builds in his throat and his pulse is racing to get out of here, and yet something deep inside orders him to stand his ground. He takes a deep breath, holds her clear blue eyes, and begins again. 'I know it sucks, what Marshal Dawe is doing, but I was wondering whether you'd like to do something this evening. Maybe we could hit the arcade or check out the pictures together, on a kind of . . .'

But before he can get that crucial word out, and establish that this is a date, Kat says: 'Sure,' so quickly it doesn't seem real. Then she looks at the drawings one more time, and crushes them into a ball. 'I guess an evening out will take my mind off things,' she adds, and shoots the ball into the bin pen.

Next her attention travels to the wedge of wasteland visible between two of the blocks. 'That was where I first met you guys,' she reminds him. 'When my family moved here this wasn't just a new city to me, it was a whole new world. Still you helped me make it feel like home, and that's always going to mean a lot to me.' She stops there, lost in thought, before batting away the moment with one hand and a sad smile. 'I know you're right though, Jude. There's nothing more we can do. It's time to move on.'

At first, he is lost for words. His invitation wasn't intended as a noble gesture, but that's how she's just read it. 'We did our best,' is all he can think to say, but even then he knows that isn't strictly true. Kat, perhaps, had made the most of her skills to get the lowdown on the Marshal, while Spinner's motor mouth had got him through the doors of City Hall, but what had Jude done to contribute? Worrying that his mum had spotted him in the sushi bar wasn't exactly something to shout about, and though Kat doesn't seem fussed, it makes it hard for him to stand proud right now.

'Drop by at eight,' she says. 'I can't stop now. My stepmother's expecting me back with some sea salt and rosemary in the next five minutes. She's cooking up something from her recipe book, and if I don't get to the store before it shuts for the day then our tea is history.' She begins to step away from Jude now, seemingly unaware that this is not quite how he had hoped things would turn out. 'Mind you, I don't have much of an appetite at the moment, and I blame Marshal Dawe for that.'

'Same here,' says Jude, but doesn't move as Kat turns to cross the car park. He doesn't blink, breathe, doesn't do anything. He knows he should be floating on air, but she's left him with a heart that just feels heavy.

eleven

'Why the long face?'

Jude drops his knapsack on the mat and finds his mum looking quizzically at him from the kitchen. She's sitting at the breakfast bar with a cup of tea and a cigarette that's always supposed to be her last. 'Please don't tell me you're in trouble at school, Jude. I had to leave work early this afternoon because your brother got caught skateboarding in the hall. His headmistress went bonkers!'

'Why? That's not so bad.'

'He was trying to jump six kids from the nursery class.' She stops there so he can think about the implications, takes a drag like she's dependent on the tube for oxygen. 'Sam persuaded them to lie down in front of some makeshift ramp, but he only got half way.'

'Ouch.'

'Luckily the only casualty was his pride, but please don't encourage him to take silly risks on that thing. It's bad enough having *one* son with no respect for heights. I don't want two of you risking life and limb every day.' She takes another hit on her cigarette, eyeing him from behind the glowing ember. 'So, are you going to tell me what's on your mind?'

Jude begins to wish he'd stayed out a little longer. He can't hide much from his mum, and he really doesn't need an interrogation now. 'It's nothing,' he says, heading for his bedroom. There's no way he's going to avoid telling her about tonight, however, which is why he steels himself to mention it at the very last moment. With his back turned, and one hand on the door handle, he goes for the casual, almost-forgot approach. 'Mum, if I do my homework now, is it OK if I go out this evening?'

'Who with?'

'Just a friend.' Jude screws his eyes shut in the hope that she won't press him further, but knows damn well that she'll never let it rest there.

'Friend in what sense? Idiot friends like Spinner and Crash? I swear I saw one of them outside City Hall today.'

'Not them, no.'

'Has one of them got a job delivering pizza?' she continues, prompting Jude to shrink inside his skin. 'You can't quit school and get a job at your age, so don't get any ideas, mister.'

'It isn't Spinner or Crash.'

'So, who *are* you seeing tonight?

With a sigh, he turns to face her. Wasn't it obvious he was talking about a girl? 'It's Katya,' he says plainly. 'I sort of asked her out.'

'You did!' She plunges the cigarette into the ashtray, her face lit up now as she twists the butt this way and that. 'That's fantastic news! Her stepmother is such a wonderful lady. Can't understand a word she says, but she always smiles when I see her. So, where are you planning on going for this . . . this *date*?'

Jude opens his mouth to say he hasn't thought that far ahead, but his mum is on a roll. 'You be sure to pack an umbrella,' she continues, 'because there's rain coming in this evening and I don't want to be responsible if she catches a chill. She's so nice, that girl. Gave me the creeps when I first met her, but just lovely underneath—'

'Mum!' Jude is finding this hard enough as it is without the quickfire questions and the overprotective comments. 'It's not even a date, really.'

'You asked her out. It's a date.'

'Yeah, but I'm not so sure she understood it like that. Losing the wasteland kind of got in the way.'

This time his mum doesn't respond immediately, but when she does it's clear she's considered every word he just said.

'Jude, I don't want to lose the wasteland any more than you. I'd rather look out at an open space than a recycling plant, but sometimes things just change.' She pauses there, considers him for a second. 'I guess you know all about changes, at your age.'

She doesn't allow him to look away when she says this,

and Jude knows what she's inviting him to open up about here. He's cool about chatting to his mum about most things, and yet he really doesn't want to go there when it comes to *those* kind of changes. It just wouldn't feel right. She was there to make sure he put on a fresh pair of socks on a daily basis and didn't let his grades slide all over the place. Maybe if this had been his dad Jude was facing now then he might've felt more comfortable. As it is, all he wants to do is get into his bedroom and work out why this doesn't feel like the greatest day of his life. That's the main thing bothering him now. The 'growing up' stuff his mum has just hinted at would sort itself out. Most probably every other boy his age was going through the same aches and insecurities. Even those flashes when it seemed that he might just be capable of anything was likely to be a hormone thing. Marvin had made him realise that he wasn't alone in feeling like a freak and the big guy had more reason to worry than most.

Jude blinks back into focus, aware that his mother's concern has prompted her to reach for yet another cigarette.

'I'd better get on with my homework,' he says, smiling for her benefit.

'If you ever need to talk, Jude, I'll do my best to help.'

'I know.'

He retreats into his room now, finds the last of the sun streaming through his window. The blinds are only half open, dividing the light so that everything is cast in stripes. He turns to close the door but pays no attention to the way the stripes slip across it, for he's struck by a sight so startling that it takes his breath clean away.

He's looking directly at the panelling in the door . . . and he can see right through it!

Jude steps back a pace, but his mother remains visible to him. It's a little fuzzy round the edges, as if the setting sun has transformed the door into a veil, but he can see enough to know he's not imagining this. Even when he wheels around to snap the blinds shut, he knows that cigarette she's smoking won't leave her looking any less sad or helpless.

Some days Jude can look at an exercise book and see nothing but a blur of words. It's supposed to be International English, but this evening it looks more like Martian the way his mind keeps wandering. That's how it is for the next ninety minutes. He just doesn't feel right, especially since that vision thing kicked in again. He had been shaken up like this the first time his senses surprised him, out in the storm drain when he could clearly see Katya approaching in his mind's eye. It only lasted a second or so this time, but isn't something he can just shrug off. *It must be stress playing tricks on me*, he thinks. What with losing the wasteland, and then Kat assuming he wanted to go out with her tonight just so they could feel better about the situation, things were seriously beginning to get on top of him.

The way he's feeling, there's no way he's going to make the right impression on her, and that just winds him up even more. He's been building the courage to ask her out for months, but now it seems as if Marshal Dawe has messed things up for him. The man might have had other motives for reclaiming the wasteland, but right now Jude feels like holding him personally responsible for what can only be a date disaster. He keeps glancing at the clock above his mirror, and can't stop thinking time is running out – but for what? His mum had been right. He needs to talk, but doesn't know where to start, and she'd only blame herself for some of the things going on inside his head.

He sighs to himself, feeling cut off from the world around and with his homework stirring up yet more stress. All he has for company is the radio: a street-tuff showcase of dub-driven cuts with Benjamin toasting over the top – and that's when he hits upon a good reason to get out of here.

Sam is wolfing down his tea when his brother emerges from his bedroom. Jude stands there with his knapsack slung over one shoulder, but the books inside have been replaced by spray cans. Not that he intends to use them. The weight just feels better on his back. As planned, he's changed into clean clothes – the hoodie and the combat pants – and his spiked hair glistens with a fresh hold of wax. Sam peers up from his plate. 'Look at you,' he says with his mouth full, 'all dressed down for your big night.'

'Shut it, stuntman. Where's Mum?'

Sam nods towards the bathroom, says she's taking a soak in the tub.

'Tell her I'll be back in good time, OK?' Jude collects his board, but stops short of the door when a voice pipes up behind him.

'Where are you going? Can I come with you?'

Jude glances over his shoulder, only to be met by a cheeky grin from his brother that tells him this is his idea of a good joke.

'Believe me, Sam,' he says, 'I don't even know where I'm going myself.'

twelve

The kid from the newspaper has just about had enough of this long afternoon. It's getting unnaturally dark but he's still with Marshal J Dawe, riding back in his limo at last. He had figured the interview would finish at the cemetery gates, but after that encounter with the vagrant the Marshal insisted that he treat him to a burger and fries. From that moment on, the man conducted himself like the kind of dad who only shows up once in a blue moon and spoils his children rotten.

The meal hadn't settled well in his stomach, however, nor the subsequent tour of the West's architectural landmarks: the giant rodeo ring that people likened to a UFO, the Museum of Advanced Art, where the pictures were exhibited on the *outside* of the building, and the front door remained permanently locked – oh yeah, that was public money well spent – then finally to the college campus they had going out there. The place stunned the young reporter. Every classroom had a bank of computers, one for every pupil, while the library went down *six* levels. Compared to this, his school just couldn't compete. The teachers did their best under the circumstances, but when you're sharing one textbook between ten pupils things got a little tough. And now the man in charge of the budgets was right here beside him, cracking each of his knuckles in turn.

'What do you say, Scoop? Today has been an education, hasn't it?'

'It certainly has, sir.' The kid is virtually on autopilot as he answers. Dawe hasn't listened to anything he's said all day, so he doesn't suppose it matters. 'I learned a great deal.' A great deal that wouldn't make it to print, he's saddened to conclude.

Witnessing all that luxury has made his blood boil – not that he dares to share this with his host. It just seems so unjust when there are streets in the East which have gone back to sharing a toilet because the sanitation out there is so ancient.

Rain has begun to spot on the windshield up front, but the chauffeur doesn't bother with his wipers. He's concentrating on driving the vehicle both swiftly and comfortably through the traffic, precisely as the Marshal has instructed. At this rate, thinks the kid from the paper, he'll be home in no time, though that hope fades when the limo pulls up several minutes later, at the foot of the steps to City Hall.

'OK, Scoop, I'll say goodbye here. Marshal J Dawe can't spend all afternoon away from the office without this city suffering. I have work to do.'

It's only when the Marshal gets out and holds open the door that the kid realises he's expected to get out, too. He can hear the man drumming his fingernails on the car roof.

'Oh,' squeaks the kid. 'I was hoping I might get a ride home. It's getting kind of late and my mum will be worrying.' It's then he catches the chauffeur's eyes in the rear view mirror, sees him wincing at what he's just asked for here. He leans out to find the Marshal's face glowering like the thunderclouds overhead, and ducks from the car so quickly he almost trips.

Gee, here's a guy who can turn off the charm.

He thanks the chauffeur anyway, then tries not to yelp when the Marshal shakes his hand. He has a powerful grip. It's as intense as the stare that he levels at him. For a beat, the kid thinks his fingers are going to get crushed, so he's even more relieved when Dawe lets him go and marches up the steps. With his hand still throbbing, he turns to cross the street – anxious to get away now. On the other side, he checks his trouser pockets but comes back with nothing but fluff. Without money for the overhead train or even a phone call home, he's just going to have to walk it.

The kid from the newspaper flips up the collar of his first ever suit, and wraps the lapels of his jacket over his camera. It's a long way back from here on foot, and he wishes that he'd packed a raincoat. What he does have is his street smarts however, and money can't buy that. As he crosses the first of many blocks, heading into the gusting wind, he knows he's going to have to keep his camera out of sight if he plans to get home in one piece.

thirteen

Marvin was right about the weather, his mother too. As Jude clears the ladder that takes him on to the roof of his block, it seems the sun hasn't set but fled from the day. It's still light, just about, but the clouds that have crept in from the East are beginning to form a malevolent brew. Even the air has a charge which makes the hairs on his neck stand on end – though that could be down to the drop Jude faces should he trip up on the short approach to *CHANNEL ZERO*.

This time he finds the door to the shack is ajar. Standing on the stoop, Jude considers knocking but then figures he can't compete against the speakers. The bass bin alone is currently shaking every timber and nail. Honestly, he thinks, on stepping inside, Benjamin plays it so loud up here on the skyline that you wonder who he's hoping to reach.

'Hey now, it's the boy with the hottest date in the city!'

Jude ducks into the studio to find Ben is busy as ever behind the turntables. Nothing much has changed since he last saw the man but for the build-up of polystyrene coffee cups beside the mixing desk.

On seeing Jude, the pirate DJ slips off one earphone, slams down the microphone fader, and invites him to take a seat. Jude, however, wants some answers before he accepts.

'What you just said,' he points out. 'How did you know Kat had agreed to go out with me?'

'The elevator may not take me high enough to get home, but I *always* keep one ear to the ground. Now shut up, sit down, and tell me how I can help.'

Jude sighs and finds the bench. How Ben knows all this stuff is a mystery, but before he opens up as requested he double checks the microphone really has been properly shut off. He's been here enough times to know how everything works, and the prospect of broadcasting his troubles across the airwaves really doesn't appeal to him right now. Even with this listening ear, in fact, Jude finds it hard to know how to start. Which is perhaps why Ben makes a fresh selection from the vinyl behind him and suggests they step out on to the stoop and talk there.

'It's an extended dub work out,' he says, cueing up the record. 'At a time like this, it's always good to have a long player to hand. Now, go fix up a jug of lime cordial, and I'll join you in a moment. Just gotta tell it to the people first, 'less they miss my wise words and start callin' up the station.'

* * *

The view from the stoop presents one of two worlds. Look West in this light, with the streetlamps beginning to pop on already, you could be fooled into thinking this city was some kind of vast circuit board, with roads and rails for wiring and scrapers in places of silicon chips. It's a different story to the East. Apart from the stuff that has been dumped or dropped, nature still rules the roost out there. When Benjamin Three-Sixty shuffles out into the open, he finds Jude facing into the wind gusting off the wasteland. The old man eases into the rocker behind the boy and closes his eyes for a moment. He could be travelling at a hundred miles an hour in that favourite seat of his, the way his dreadlocks flail and snap behind him. Wherever he's heading behind those heavy lids, Ben seems to be enjoying the journey.

'It's about time the rain fell,' he says, looking up now to take in the bruised and clotted clouds. 'This city needs to freshen up every once in a while, just as we do. Leave it too long and the place starts to stink. Man, I want to wake up tomorrow morning and breathe in good clean air.'

'I just want to wake up tomorrow morning,' sighs Jude. 'Right now I feel like skipping this date and forgetting I ever asked Kat to go out with me. At least then I could move on.'

'Oh, you *think*?' Ben's sarcasm draws Jude around now. 'Boy, if you blow her out you'll never forgive yourself. She's expecting you, no?'

'In about half an hour, but I can't let go of the fact we're about to lose the wasteland and I've done nothing to stop that. It makes me feel like a failure, Ben, and if I feel that way then Kat's bound to take the same view.'

'Either way, she's going to feel worse if you just vanish on her.'

Jude thinks about it, Ben seemingly searching his gaze for something, and once again the memory of his father forms like a ghost inside his mind. That's when this ageing DJ with the snaking dreads begins to smile and nod, as if he too can see the man taking shape behind the boy's eyes. Jude reflects on the question some more. Finally, he says, 'I don't want to let anyone down, Ben, myself included.'

'You'll be fine, so long as you follow my advice and stick with your two steps.'

'Er, that didn't quite work out.' Jude drops his attention to the planks underfoot. 'My first step was to look my best when I talked to her, but then I bumped into her before I'd had a chance to get ready. Everything went pear-shaped from there.'

'You think it makes a difference to her that you're wearing yesterday's socks? If a girl's genuinely into you, Jude, it won't matter if you asked her out all dressed up like you've been dragged through a hedge backwards. Which, by the way, is exactly how you appear to me right now.'

'It's a look,' Jude protests, aware that even this wind can't defeat his spikes.

'Couldn't you at least pull your trousers up some? If you let them hang any lower they're going to fall off your waist completely.'

'Ben! The fact is I've blown it with Kat because I don't feel good enough for her, and it's all because of Marshal Dawe.'

'So deal with it. Do everything in your power to save the wasteland, I guarantee you'll hold your head up high.'

'It's too late. We're expecting the bulldozers tomorrow, and even if there *is* dirt on Dawe that might put a stop to this development, he's got it locked up in that dome of his on top of City Hall.'

'All you have to do is give this your very best shot. Doesn't matter what the outcome is, you'll come back knowing more about yourself than ever before.'

'You're talking to Jude here,' he reminds the old man. 'My dad may have been the one who made out he could pull off miracles, but not me. I'm a realist, Ben. I've been that way since he left us in the lurch all those years back.'

'Even realists need to keep an open mind,' Ben insists, ice-cool as always. He could be sitting out in the sun, the way he relaxes in his rocker. The old man doesn't even blink when thunder rolls through the cloud mass. 'Jude, this is your chance to find out what makes you tick, and I know that's been troubling you for some time. It's why you're here, after all.'

Jude doesn't know what to say, mostly because he can't dispute what Ben has just said. Then he thinks: *What have I got to lose?* and a spark comes into his expression that Ben seems pleased to see.

'It's a shame you're not my dad,' Jude jokes next. 'Dads are supposed to have this kind of chat with their sons, after all. I still think what you're asking me to do is impossible, though. City Hall is a high-security building, and so far our best efforts have got us no further than the lobby – but if you say it's the only way forward, then I'll do it. I guess because I respect your word.'

Ben listens to the boy, and swallows hard when he's finished. Finally, he breaks off with a private smile for the sky and says: 'Your daddy would be proud of you, man.'

'I'm not doing it for him.' Jude crosses the stoop to collect his board now, looking stung all of a sudden. 'Ben, the guy came home with presents as well as stories, like he could buy our affection!'

'No matter how much hurt he caused, it doesn't mean he stopped caring for you one little bit.'

'If he cared for me, he'd still be here today.'

'Maybe he is,' Ben says under his breath.

Jude stops in his tracks, as if a spell has just been cast on him, while the old man continues to sit contentedly in his rocker doing that wise-or-whacked-out thing you can get away with at his age.

'Is there something I should be told?' asks Jude.

'Nope,' Ben replies, quite casually, 'but there's a whole lot you can find out for yourself if you put your heart into saving the wasteland. Consider it your new first step, and let the next step take care of itself.'

Ben doesn't need to state that he's talking about a date. This much is crystal clear to Jude, unlike the small problem of how he's actually going to gain access to the penthouse space that crowns a guarded building. All this talk of doing your best and pushing yourself to the limit didn't count for much when faced with some knucklehead in a security guard's uniform.

'So, where do I start?' he asks, bemused, and looks around like he's missing something.

Benjamin eases himself from the rocker and rises to his feet. He too scans the mountainous city skyline, the summit pricking the cloud shelf. Then he swings right round, and his attention falls with great purpose upon the adjacent tower block. 'Over there,' he says, nodding at the flat rooftop, much to the boy's astonishment.

'Huh? I was hoping you were going to tip me off about how to blag my way into City Hall.'

'I am,' he says, rising to his feet now. 'I hear your friend Spinner proved there's only one way into that building, starting from the top.' He gestures at the neighbouring roof once more. 'So I'm thinking if you can cross that divide, you'll never look back.'

Jude's first response is to laugh, even if the old man's comic timing could be better. But Ben's expression doesn't shift. He's deadly serious, prompting panic to crash over the boy in waves. He turns to size up the challenge, astonished to be put in this position, and yet deep down he senses that it's possible. A ten-metre jump, with a full run from the foot of the stoop to the ramp-like lip of the building, and he should have enough speed on his side to clear the gap. On the ground he wouldn't think twice about attempting a stunt like this – it's just a little suicidal from this height. If he messes up here, he'll have a lot more than two grazed knees to worry about. There'll be no second chance, no date, no life to live.

'I dunno,' he says nervously, as the man comes to stand at his side, 'that's some leap of faith.'

'That, my friend, is *exactly* what it is.' Ben pauses there for another battery of thunder. 'All you have to do is believe in yourself, like we believe in you.'

'*We?*'

'It'll all make sense from the other side,' Ben assures him, and steps back quietly so Jude can take the stage.

fourteen

A lightning strike is triggered by an electric charge: a massive build-up of positive and negative energy that combines to unleash the big bolt out of nowhere. Jude can sense it coming, but not just in the way the storm clouds begin to seethe and boil. Preparing for this, the biggest jump of his life, he can also feel it right here beneath one foot. He rolls the board back and forth, his eyes fixed on the concrete ravine ahead. Every hope he's ever held out for seems to strain against the sadness and resentment from his past, and somehow this only serves to fuel his determination. Positive and negative, rolled into one. *If my father could see me now*, he thinks to himself, *I wouldn't know whether to hug him or kick his ass*.

There's no more time to dwell on things, for in the same breath that electrical charge goes critical and a jagged bolt spits at the earth. The strike hits a car wreck in the wasteland, much closer than the last one, causing sparks to crackle and shower. It startles the old man on the stoop, who takes his eye off the boy for a moment. And, when Ben looks back, he sees Jude has begun his journey.

'*Go, my friend, GO!*'

The boy doesn't take his eye off the chasm he has to cross. Even the blistering thunderclap can't distract Jude now he's rushing towards the edge of the building. He's putting so much into his approach that by rights the wheels should be matching the bone-jarring rumble overhead, but he doesn't hear a thing. Can't even sense the wheels connecting.

'*NOW, Jude . . .*'

The final few feet come at him so quickly that he couldn't change his mind now even if he wanted to. Then the board hits the lip and lifts abruptly over the abyss. Jude crouches on instinct, grips the edge of the deck to stop it from falling away, and feels somehow that he's left his body behind. It's his *soul* out here on the board: an untouchable force just like the second lightning bolt to lash out from the clouds, so close this time that everything goes white for a split-second.

It's only when Jude ducks this jagged fork of energy that he sees the second block coming right at him: looking very real yet just too far away. The board begins to succumb to gravity, the roof of the tower block tips out of view but Jude just hangs on in there, willing himself to make it. If he misses he'll be mincemeat, and his heart flies into his mouth as if to seek refuge should he fall.

With his free hand the boy reaches out now towards the next ledge, almost willing it closer through his fingertips before bailing from his board because he *knows* that he can make it . . .

'. . . *fly!*'

Jude doesn't exactly finish with the same grace and ambition that marked his launch. In fact, the tumble he takes makes it look like he's just been chucked over there like a rag doll. What matters is the knowledge that he's *survived* this spectacular wipe-out, because when the deck follows on and catches his calf muscle it causes him to yelp out loud. The pain can't match his elation, however. No way. He climbs to his feet to see where he's come from but he just can't take it in. In fact, it's the figure on the other side of the gulf who has to spell it out for him. Benjamin Three-Sixty is standing dangerously close to the other edge himself now, and Jude wonders whether he had chased behind him right up to the moment he jumped.

'You made it!' Ben cups his mouth to be heard over the sheeting wind, and then punches the air with both fists. 'That was out of this world, man! *Unbelievable!*'

Jude can barely take it in himself. All he can be sure of is that he feels very different indeed. He still can't quite believe he had the guts to give it a shot, but right now he senses that he's capable of *anything*. Was that why Ben had encouraged him to jump? The old man had seemed so certain Jude could make it.

Then he thinks some more, and a long-smouldering question ignites once more in his mind. Across the divide, beyond this deadly drop, he finds Ben's gaze and holds it. 'Those stories my dad used to tell me,' he shouts over. 'He always swore blind that he could do stuff nobody would believe.'

'So maybe you shouldn't think of them as stories any more, Jude.'

'Are you saying he was telling the truth? I always thought he was covering for the fact that he'd been out boozing!'

Rain begins spotting then spitting, coming down harder and harder, but Jude stands his ground, holding out for a response. Finally, the man with all the answers takes a step back, like his time out here is almost done.

'He's your daddy, Jude. Nothing can change that, whatever he became when you were younger.'

'Yeah, but a *superhero*? C'mon, Ben. What are we talking about here? Captain Whisky-Breath? The Incredible Drunk?'

'Not all heroes have fancy names or costumes! Most just do the best they can with what they have. But let me tell you, Jude, even superheroes have their problems, exactly like you and me.' What Ben relays across the gap hits Jude hard. Everything he's ever held against his father just falls away like the rain between these two blocks.

'Some say having special powers is a gift,' Ben bellows, 'but it can be a curse if you're not careful. All that responsibility you have to make the world a safer place? It creates a lot of pressure. We both know that talking helps get problems in perspective, but what can you do when nobody knows who you really are? That's why your daddy took to the bottle, Jude. He thought drinking would help him escape every now and then, but it proved to be his greatest enemy.'

'He walked out on his family!' snaps Jude.

'And just look what he left behind!' the old man yells back, one hand outstretched towards the boy now. 'This is just the beginning for you, boy. It's your time now!'

Jude kicks his skateboard upright, rests his foot on the deck once again, but this time the buzz that follows doesn't feel weird at all. It seems perfectly natural, in fact, as if perhaps it's something he might have inherited. Of all the changes he's been going through, from the squeaky voice to the shiny skin, this is one that leaves him standing proud.

'So where do I go from here?' The storm is really coming on strong now, and the wind threatens to sweep Jude's questions away.

'Just follow your heart,' Ben shouts back, and pauses there just long enough for Jude to consider the two burning issues in his life right now. When it looks as if the boy has registered what needs to be done, this cracked old man throws his hands to the sky. 'It's all there for you, Jude!' he yells, as lightning slashes over the city behind him. 'The further you go, the more you'll discover about yourself.'

'What about my father?' Jude calls out, but the man seems to have finished now. He's turning already, heading for the shelter of his shack. All Jude wants to ask, the one big question, is whether his dad is dead or alive. That sense of power he gets from his skateboard is beginning to peak once again, however, and it draws him back to the task at hand. He glances at his wristwatch, and catches his breath when he sees the time. For he's running late for his date now, and in view of his new plans for this evening, he's also completely unprepared.

Damn right, I need some special powers, he thinks to himself, pulling up his hood. *Special powers of persuasion*.

fifteen

When her mobile phone announces that a text has just arrived, Katya is putting the finishing touches to her face. Once she's done with her eyes, any boy would be mad to look into them for longer than a blink.

Except for maybe one lad she really likes. A buff kind of guy who has only just started to find himself in her presence.

She hasn't had much time to get ready for this evening out with Jude, as her step-mum had insisted she eat at the table. The woman had only married her dad a couple of years earlier, but right from the start she was determined that things were done right. 'No matter what plans you might have,' she always said, 'the family who eats together, stays together.' She was OK, her step-mum. A bit strict, but her heart was in exactly the right place.

Kat leaves the message unread for a minute, fixes her hair, then grabs the phone. Her eyes scan the text and go back again. Checking she's understood it right. Scowling, she calls back the number. It barely rings before someone picks up.

'*Kat, I can explain—*'

'Jude Ash! Did you really think you could slide out of tonight by *text* message? I thought you were different, but you're such a typical boy! What's going on? Why d'you want to cancel?'

'*I don't want to cancel. It's just . . . listen, my studies have caught up with me and, um, I'm going to need a little extra time on it.*'

'What do you need? An hour?'

Her question is met by a long silence. Nothing but the sound of static in her ear and the rain drumming against her bedroom window. Finally, she hears Jude take a deep breath.

'*I was thinking maybe a day.*'

'I see.' She winces, trying hard not to sound hurt. This is Katya he's messing with here, after all, and there's no way she's going to let on how disappointed she feels all of a sudden. She'd been through a lot in her life before coming to this city, but she isn't as strong as people think.

'*Please, Kat, you have to trust me on this.*'

'I guess it's a crappy night to be going out anyway,' she says with a sigh, one eye on the weather outside. 'Anyway,' she finishes breezily, like this isn't such a big deal for her, 'what are you studying?'

'*Modern architecture,*' is what he says, which surprises her, considering they don't study that subject at school. It sounds like a very shifty story indeed, but Jude had asked her to trust him, and that's all she can do.

Had she known where Jude was calling from, it would have made more sense. For the boy isn't in his bedroom, but on the summit of a building in the heart of the city. He isn't looking at textbooks, either, but at a building topped by a big glass dome – one with a figure at work inside it.

Jude snaps shut his phone and stows it in the knapsack on his back. He's soaked through to the skin, but his concern goes way beyond the storm. His focus didn't shift when he made the call, but now it becomes more intense. He narrows his eyes, choosing to ignore where he is and what might happen if he makes one wrong move. Inside the dome, the man moves out of sight every now and then, usually to charge his glass from the mini-bar he has hidden behind a potted palm, and yet Jude tracks every unseen movement. It's a strange sensation, same as it had been on the wasteland and in his bedroom earlier.

Only this time he's content to just let the feeling flow through him. However long it takes for this guy to finish his work for the night, he's prepared to wait. It doesn't help that Jude is crouched on one of the many sloping outcrops that make up the neighbouring building: a showy metropolitan hotel with ledges, spires, and neon-lit parapets. Some said it looked like a castle, cathedral and

Christmas tree rolled into one, but all that concerns Jude now is that it's higher than City Hall by a storey or so. Despite the risk to life and limb, Jude is committed to seeing this through. Not just for his sake, but for everyone that means something to him – and that includes his dad.

The building wasn't difficult to scale. Anyone could've done it really. All it took was courage, a lot of it, mostly in slipping past the bus boy to gain access to the elevator. From there, it was just a question of riding to the observation deck at the very top. The tricky bit came once he'd climbed over the suicide-nets, and then used his skateboard to switch down the slate slopes until he was directly overlooking the Marshal at his desk.

Jude had never been snowboarding, but he figured this wasn't much different from the descent techniques some of the extreme guys used out on the mountaintops. The only thing that seriously differed was what might happen if he slipped or a tile gave way underneath him now.

'Don't even think about it,' he tells himself, having just glanced over the parapet he's wedged behind. All he can see down below is a thin string of red and yellow lights. Knowing that's traffic at street level is enough to make his head spin. A flock of pigeons are sheltering from the downpour in a nook just above him, but they could sail out of here if they slipped into trouble. Without wings, Jude has yet to test what would happen if he took a jump too far on his board. What he *does* possess is self-belief: an inner confidence that had come from his leap between the two blocks. Even if that was down to special powers, Jude can only guess how far it might take him. All he knows is that right now it feels absolutely right to be here: as a force for the greater good in a city with corruption at its core.

Frowning at his monitor, Marshal J Dawe thumps his desk and curses the name of the stupid kid from the newspaper. All afternoon it had taken to be sure he hadn't read anything into that little scene in the park. Dawe really didn't want him running home to write up some story about his policy for dealing with drunks. *All afternoon*, until finally his patience had run dry!

In that time, broods the Marshal, he could've leaned on that construction company to start work on the wasteland as they had promised. After everything he had done to make sure they landed the contract for the recycling plant, what did they do but delay by a day! It wasn't good enough, and Dawe had assured them he would be there in person first thing tomorrow morning to be sure they began work on time. Cutting through the red tape to make sure Cactus Industries landed the contract had been no easy task, and for that he expected some payback.

First off, they'd get the job done on time, so it would look good in the press.

Secondly, Cactus would keep their mouths shut about the fact that he had purchased a whole bunch of shares on behalf of his son. Setting up Jack Junior with his very own company, Sheriff Holdings, had been the Marshal's brainchild. The idle boy didn't even know he was Managing Director, probably couldn't spell it either. All it had taken was a little paperwork and, hey presto, Sheriff Holdings was open for business and picking up shares in a construction company that could only rise in value.

Buying into Cactus, knowing that they would be sure to land the contract for the wasteland, meant the value of each share had rocketed. Naughty, really, he supposed. Very bad business practice. OK, completely illegal, but a sly move that would see him profit nicely. And even if someone was smart enough to sniff around (though who would bother over that crappy scrap of land?), the Marshal is safe in the knowledge that it would be his son who took the punishment and not him. That slacker good-for-nothing boy deserved a short, sharp shock anyhow, and if it meant a spell in a youth correctional facility then so be it. What's more, when the son of a public figure fell from grace people usually felt sympathy for the family. He thinks through the consequences should this unfortunate situation arise, and feels much better for it. For that sympathy could only translate into votes come the next election, bringing him yet another term in an office he has almost made his own.

Reflecting on the plan makes him feel much better, and he leans forward to continue working at his computer. Marshal J Dawe has not got where he is today without knowing how to cover his tracks. No, sir! One time there had been a man who threatened to expose his little dealings on the side. This guy was blessed with an uncanny ability to show up at the wrong time, usually when Dawe was involved in something that would see him kicked out of office. On a couple of occasions he'd almost been rumbled completely, and that would've surely been the case had the fool not started sinking too many beers. *Which is what happens when you think you can outwit Marshal J*, he thinks, and considers pouring himself one more Scotch to toast his good fortune. Whenever he runs into big problems in his life, why, he just pays for them to be overcome. Drinking yourself silly was a loser's game, and there were plenty of drunks drifting around the city to remind him of that. Everywhere he went, it seemed, some lush would lurch out of nowhere. Almost always it reminded him of the guy who used to make a more dramatic appearance, which is perhaps what stops Dawe from stamping all over them. That earlier encounter in the park was no exception, if a little embarrassing with the kid from the newspaper present.

Reflecting on this for a moment, he makes a mental note to have his law men crack down hard on vagrants just as soon as this current venture is complete. Using two fingers, he stabs at the keyboard, checks Cactus' share price is still rising nicely, and concludes that it really is time to head home.

The Marshal leans back in his leather swivel chair, and consults each armpit with a good long sniff. Holy Moley, it had been a long day, but as the floor below is host to a gym, a sauna and showers it's impossible for him to leave the building looking less than perfect.

He rises from the chair, grinning to himself as he heads for the spiral stairwell. Cleaning up was what he enjoyed most about this life, after all. Not just the kind you did under a hot jet of water, but the type that involved making lots and *lots* of money.

sixteen

From the rooftop overlooking the glass dome, Jude watches the man sink from view – step by slow-turning step. The Marshal even dims the lights in the dome as he leaves, which makes the monitor on his desk appear to burn all the more brightly.

'About time,' the boy mutters to himself. Easing out from behind the parapet, Jude begins to inch across the glistening, rain-lashed slates. The pigeons up here watch his progress with cocked heads and beady eyes, unsure what this boy is doing as he lowers his feet over the guttering to find the ledge just below. Compared to the blocks back at The Projects, there's less of a gap between these two buildings, but the drop down to the dome looks potentially fatal. Like, how many skaters in their right mind were prepared to make a leap on to *glass*?

Jude reaches for a pocket in his combat trousers, finds a crumpled ball of paper. As he flattens out the sheet on his thigh, it releases a faint trace of patchouli – the favourite scent of the girl who had last handled it. Before travelling into the city he had stopped by at the bin pen and rooted out the architect's drawings that Kat discarded earlier. She may have believed this downloaded document was useless at the time, but Jude would not be without it now.

He scours the plans, confirming that the escape hatch at the very top of the dome is the best point of entry. That's if he's to avoid the attention of the security team or the intruder alarms on all the floors below. Once inside, it's just a question of finding the right file on the Marshal's computer, then using his wits to climb out again.

Hmmm, he thinks, waking up to the reality of his plan. *A regular walk in the park.*

Jude is just dwelling on the wisdom of this crazy leap once again when a gust of wind snatches the document from his hands, whipping it up and out of his reach. Helplessly, the boy watches it twist away into the dark, thinking *There goes any other option*. Then he reconsiders, aware that he has to stay positive, and decides it's a sign that this is the only way forward from here.

Without looking down again, he reaches for his board and psyches himself up with a countdown:

'Five . . . four . . .'

Marshal J Dawe stands on the cold porcelain tiles, naked but for his ten-gallon hat. It's the last thing he takes off before stepping into the shower cubicle, revealing a bald crown that's never been seen in public. His hair is thick at the back and sides, just so it looks like there's more going on beneath his hat when the cameras are switched on. Right now, however, it simply looks like an emperor's laurels that have slipped a little too much. As soon as he spins the taps, the steam begins to rise in blankets. The Marshal whistles as he washes, looking forward to putting his feet up at home, maybe watching some sport before bed. Had he known that someone was about to make a surprise entrance one floor up from here, the steam would most probably be coming out of his ears.

'. . . three . . . two . . . *one*!'

Jude throws himself on to his skateboard, pushing out as hard as he can. At the same time, his mind snaps back to that first weird trick he'd pulled in the wasteland. Then Marvin swore the boy had beaten gravity, going right against nature, and Jude knows that he needs to find the same kind of airtime if this isn't to be his last leap ever. The board beneath his feet could have a heartbeat of its own, but no matter how alive it makes Jude feel, the crown of that dome still races up to meet him. Gathering speed now, and dropping fast, he clings to the edge of his deck with one hand, his free arm raised high like this is a bull steer he's riding.

'Bring it on!' he instructs himself, desperate to find that magic as the seconds fall away. '*Uh-oh!*' He screws shut his eyes, clinging to the thought that he really doesn't want to die, and prays the impact will make it quick. The rain on his back plus the violent up-rush of wind don't make this plunge any easier, nor the string of memories that hurtle through his mind now. It could be a show-reel of his life, unravelling from this moment back: the dark day his dad left plays out in a flash, then the golden years before all that, when the guy was fit to call himself a father. That's what Jude misses most, and such is the force of emotions this triggers he could be right here with him again. The moment doesn't last, however. It comes to a shuddering halt, but there's no sound of splintering glass and bone to finish.

There's no sound at all, Jude realises, and dares to pop open one eye.

All around, everything seems so still. It's as if God has hit the slow-mo button, but forgotten to include the boy. Even the rain appears to be hanging in the air, and he gasps when he sees that the same thing applies to him. Looking down, he finds the glass hatch beneath the deck, but if he rocks to and fro there's definitely a cushion of air supporting him. At first Jude is too scared to make a move, as if somehow that might snap this spell he appears to be caught in.

Then he thinks, *Oh, sod it, I made it this far, didn't I?* and steps off the deck.

As he does so, the wheels clatter hard against the toughened glass. Jude whips around, and wonders whether he really could've been hovering somehow just a moment ago. There's no time to test his suspicions, however, because his senses open up more and the howling wind threatens to knock him off his perch. Whatever that was all about, it's clear to him that one wrong move from this moment on could see him splattered on a coach roof or the bonnet of a car. He sinks to his knees and finds the handle for the escape hatch. Jude pulls hard, the panel of glass lifts away seamlessly, and a wave of warm air meets his face. This time he collects the board and drops it in first, just to see what happens with his own eyes. He lets go of the tail end, watches it clatter like a dead weight on to the carpet below, and figures perhaps he needs to be on it before the out of sight stuff can happen.

'That was a dumb move,' he mutters to himself, with no choice now but to drop through the hatch and hope he lands better than his board.

'*Thwump!*'

The man in the shower stops soaping his face and takes a step back. He looks at the ceiling, wondering if his ears just deceived him. *Must be the pipes*, he decides, and returns his face to the streaming water. He even begins to hum a tune to himself, a campfire song he's picked up from watching one too many westerns. Then a second impact hits the ceiling above him, this time more forcefully, and immediately the man falls silent. He shuts off both taps, straining to listen. Finally, with a sigh, he figures he'd better go see for himself. There's stuff on that computer that he wouldn't want people to find, after all. Not even clumsy cleaning staff.

Once again, Jude has to open his eyes to check he's still alive. He finds himself spread-eagled next to his board, looking up at the hatch he's just dropped through. He wiggles his feet, his hands, and his ears, but groans as he gathers himself from the carpet. He's twisted an ankle for sure, but nursing it will have to wait until his job here is done. Hobbling to the desk now, Jude settles in front of the Marshal's computer screen, and wonders where to start looking. There are all manner of folders on the desktop, but searching through each one could take an age. He has a disk in his pocket, but it's no use without the file that lists all the shareholders. He also has his phone and considers the last time the cavalry came to his rescue, back in the City Railroad Station . . .

When Kat sees the caller's name crop up on her mobile screen, the second appearance in the same evening, she picks up straight away.

'Jude? I thought you were studying?'

'*I am, sort of, but I need some tech help.*'

'Why are you whispering?' she asks.

'*Kat,*' he continues, pressingly, '*how do you search for a file on a computer?*'

'Duh!' She has to struggle not to hoot. 'Don't you know?'

'*C'mon, just tell me how to do it. I never really clicked with computers like I do with skateboarding.*'

'You are the missing link, Jude. That is such a basic question, you doofus!'

'*Kat!*'

She sighs to herself, then chuckles at the fact that the boy who had earlier stood her up is now practically on his knees begging for advice. Still, he sounds pretty strung out, so she tells him straight how to search out a file: running through the procedure step by simple step.

'See the search box now?' she asks, as he acts on her instructions. 'You'll find it using that.'

'*I see now, that's great. I'm typing as I speak.*'

'Can I ask what you're looking for?' she says, picking up on the clattering keys. 'What's the rush?'

'*Found it!*' he tells her excitedly, and the clattering comes to a halt.

'What?'

'*Just the lowdown on Sheriff Holdings!*' That wipes the smile from Katya's face. '*What I'm looking at here is a record of who's in charge and who really calls the shots. You're going to like what you see.*'

A look of complete surprise consumes Kat for a beat, and then it all makes sense. 'Are you where I think you are?' She sounds alarmed now. 'Jude, are you OK?'

This time he doesn't respond. She's about to ask again, but it sounds like someone else is talking to him. Then he comes back on the line, and says, *'Kat, I think I'd better go.'*

seventeen

Marshal J Dawe advances slowly but surely up the spiral staircase. He's all wrapped up in a silk kimono gown with a giant dragon embroidered across the back, and topped off with his ten-gallon hat. He doesn't care what he looks like, because the only person who can see him is this skate punk who's making a phone call at his desk. He's a big man, the Marshal, but his presence seems to grow further when the boy catches sight of him. He glances up from the monitor, once, then twice, as if he can't quite believe this is happening, and suddenly seems lost for words. Even the voice on the other end of his mobile doesn't stir him into action.

'You know,' Dawe begins now, sounding horribly breezy, 'at times like this, when kids like you run wild, I *always* blame the parents.'

The boy with the spiked-up hair just freezes in his chair, but he isn't the only one who seems shocked to the core when their eyes lock. For the Marshal recognises someone else in his face. Someone all too familiar to him in the years since he rose to this office. In that moment, it's as if he's looking directly at the spirit of a man whose presence in this city once chilled him to the bone. A man who could almost be reborn right here before him.

Jude can still hear Kat calling his name on the phone. She sounds concerned but he's too stunned to speak. Why hadn't he sensed the Marshal coming? All the way in he'd been sure Dawe was on the floor below, but now here he is, live, direct and looking increasingly murderous. Jude suddenly wishes he'd collected his board from the carpet when he crossed to the desk. He doesn't feel complete without it – exposed somehow to all manner of danger.

Gathering his wits as best he can, Jude closes his call to Katya and punches out the disk from the computer.

'*Who* are you?' Marshal J Dawe growls.

Jude considers the question without really thinking. 'My father's son,' is what he says, because the one thing on his mind right now is whether he really *has* inherited his old man's powers. For if it turns out Jude has just been kidding himself all this time, pulling stupid stunts and getting lucky, then he's in *really* big trouble. Worse still, his board is over there, on the wrong side of the desk for him to make a quick escape. Jude pockets the disk, just as the Marshal advances towards him.

'Look at the mess you've made,' he tells the boy, gesturing at the rain drifting in through the open hatch. 'You'd better hope you follow in your dad's footsteps because if you can't fly out of here you'll be kissing the tarmac!'

With that, Marshal Dawe twists round to catch him unawares, but staggers as he clips the skateboard. Jude steps back on instinct, with no time to lose before the man sprawls into the desk.

Get outta here! he tells himself, scrambling to seize the board that has just saved his skin. The Marshal reaches out to grab his leg, but with the deck in Jude's possession once again that invincible buzz returns to his body. Even the ache in his ankle seems to disappear, and it feels so natural – as if this is how things should be. *Now*, he thinks, *we're in business!*

Slamming the board in front of him, Jude leaps forward to meet it with just enough time to kick up on to the rail around the spiral staircase. The underbelly of his board grinds hard against the steel bar, but Jude holds true. Fighting to keep his balance, he corkscrews towards the next level.

'You're gonna be sorry, boy!'

Jude can hear the Marshal clattering down the steps, and knows he isn't far behind. Worse still, he has no idea where to go from here, for this wasn't part of the plan and he no longer has the drawings to guide him.

The floor below is host to all kinds of personal

pampering. Wherever he looks, Jude sees nothing but fitness machines lined up like soldiers on parade. From walking to running, rowing and cycling, it's all here, but what Jude really needs is a *time* machine. Anything to rewind by a couple of minutes and avoid finding himself in this fix. Leaping from the rail now, all he can do is race for the elevator at the back and hope it takes him out of here. By now, however, the Marshal has gathered up a head of steam. Jude glances over his shoulder, sees an outstretched hand reaching for the scruff of his hoodie, and ducks with no time to spare.

The Marshal swipes at thin air, and howls in fury and frustration as Jude sweeps away. He knows here's no way he's going to make the elevator now, so what can he do? Blast through one of the gallery windows? Jude knows he's not brave or stupid enough, even if his skateboard could save him from a multi-storey drop.

He considers going back the way he came in, via the dome's glass hatch, but reaching it would involve hauling the desk underneath and placing the chair on top, and he's not strong enough to do that alone. The Marshal circles in the opposite direction, pushing around a bank of running machines in a bid to cut him off at the other end of the gym. The man really doesn't look like he'd respond well to a request to help Jude shift a heavy desk.

What would Dad have done? he asks himself in

desperation, thinking this is just like one of his old man's tall stories. Always his tales had been about saving the city from this kind of evil or that kind of threat, but Jude is lost for a happy ending of his own here. He's almost reached the far side of the gymnasium, and the Marshal is closing in on his right flank. Jude glances round, and almost whoops for joy at what he would've otherwise missed. The neon sign even spells it out for him, no special powers required.

Stairs! He'll take the stairs out of here, like any other normal human being. He bears towards this, his only means of escape – cutting just in front of the Marshal.

'Dumb move,' Jude hears him growl, way too close behind him for comfort. Furiously he drives the board faster with one foot, his shoulder braced so that when he hits the swing doors they practically fly off the hinges.

'Owww!'

The impact hurts like hell, but it's enough to carry him through. Unlike the Marshal, who finds the doors swinging back into his face. It stops him dead, but not for long. As Jude travels down the first flight of stairs, rattling over the steps because he's had no time to hit the rail, he can hear threats echoing after him. A sensor alarm starts to scream as he descends to the next level, but that can't disguise just how crazed the Marshal sounds – crazed, but somehow very sure of himself.

*'You won't escape, boy! Your father dug his own grave.
I'm about to dig yours!'*

eighteen

Finding himself alone on the gym floor, Marshal J Dawe quits yelling and takes stock of his injuries. He touches his nose, winces sharply and notes the blood that comes away on his fingertips. He dabs at it once again, finds more of the same, and his senses begin to regroup. Good Lord, his head hurts! It almost saddens him to think that the skate punk will have to pay an even higher price if his hooter looks as bad as it feels.

Despite being stunned by the impact with the closing doors, Dawe has to marvel at the boy's escape. That board of his could have been a bird, the way he'd swooped it around the foot of the first flight of steps and soared over the next, and he knows he can't catch up on foot. He narrows his eyes, thinking ahead. He can hear one sensor alarm after another kicking off as his quarry passes floor after floor. Each one triggers a siren, and the chorus of panic this creates just serves to taunt the man. This is his *building*, damn it. His *city*. He isn't going to let some wretched adolescent mess up his plans.

When the bell chimes over the elevator, the Marshal

responds like it's an idea that's just arrived in his head. He wheels around, still nursing his nose, and marches towards the doors that have just glided open. Inside, he stabs at the ground floor button, and begins to feel much better. It's going to take him what, half a minute, to reach the lobby? The only way that kid is going to make ground level before him is if he drops down the gap in the stairwell and lets gravity take over.

The three security guards are busy checking out a rodeo event on a small television behind the reception desk. The building is closed for business, this time of night, and they're sure the Marshal won't mind because he likes to keep up on who can ride a steer the best in this city.

The first thing to draw them from the screen is the commotion coming down the stairwell. First one sensor alarm, then another, and on top of all that a muffled rumbling that persuades them to reach for their holsters. These guys are pumped. There isn't much that intimidates them, but the cacophony resounding through the floors right now is enough to prompt some worried glances.

The second thing to distract them is way more troubling, however, and that's the sight of City Hall's main man emerging from the elevator wearing a flowing silk dressing-gown and his ten-gallon hat.

'Jeez,' exclaims one guard under his breath. 'And I

thought a shoestring tie was too fancy on a man.'

There's no time for his buddies to comment, however, for the Marshal is stomping across the marble floor towards them. He's sporting a pulped and bloody nose, with some bruising to his forehead too. Still, he clearly has enough fire in him to be yelling at the guards to station themselves at the foot of the stairs.

'There's an intruder in the building and I want you to stop him whatever it takes, understood?' He pauses for breath here, his nostrils flaring like a bull regrouping before his next charge. Then he gestures at their holsters, and speaks a little more privately, despite the racket. 'It's late,' he says, drawing closer. 'If the boy is involved in an accident, nobody will know.'

The guards seem surprised, but it's the guard with the comments about the Marshal's dress sense who voices his concern.

'Did you say a *boy*, sir?' He lets the Marshal listen to the wail of alarms and the rumbling that unsettles them so. 'What's he doing to make all that noise? Riding a *chariot* down the stairs?'

'In a manner of speaking, that's exactly what he's doing, now block that staircase, *right away*!'

The boy on the board has only two more levels to go before he makes the lobby. His heart is hammering, his mouth bone dry, while his ears are ringing right off the scale. All the sirens sounding in his wake are a measure of the floors he's dropped through, and it's enough to wake the dead. Now his knees are aching from having to cushion all the jolts and he's sweating through fear as well as effort. It's taken every ounce of skill to descend this far so quickly, but one wrong move and the bail-out would be brutal. Each flight of stairs switches one way then the other, though the stairwell itself is cylindrical and it's here that Jude now takes full advantage. He crouches low, clinging to the upper edge of his deck as his descent goes totally vertical. Hurtling into the final flight, he's more like a motorcyclist in a wall of death than a kid with everything to lose. Then the lobby swings into view, there at the foot of the steps, and Jude knows that in these closing seconds his chance for freedom will live or die.

Most likely the latter, he thinks, *in view of the welcome party waiting for me.*

'Here he comes!'

Jude had half-expected to find security blocking his path. What causes him to catch his breath is the sight of the other man with them – the one he'd left behind in the gymnasium – and yet there's no going back now. With so much velocity on his side, Jude rides the final wall with his eyes smarting. The figures down there are just a blur, and that's all they see of the boy as well. He can still feel that buzz but it's losing out to a sense of horror, because there's no way he's going to clear these guys.

'Do something!' the Marshal yells, and immediately the three guards draw their weapons. 'Take him *down*!'

Jude is committed now, and levels the board as the wheels leave the wall. *That's it!* He's in the air again, where it feels so right, except he's rocketing towards the man in the cowboy hat. The guards splinter in all directions, protecting themselves while attempting to draw a bead with their pistols. But Jude can only focus on one thing, and that's the glass exit behind this final obstacle.

'*Stop!!!*' is all the Marshal bellows, like *that's* going to happen, and throws up his hands. Jude doesn't want to hurt anyone here, it's not in his nature. But this is one collision he can't avoid. All he can do is tip the nose of his board up so that the four wheels connect with the Marshal's chest. *Bam!* The man goes down like an old lady on ice, no match for this boy as he powers into the lobby. The guards? They just can't keep him in their sights for long enough to shoot, and when the boy heads straight ahead they simply stand and stare.

The rain is still falling hard outside, but the thunder and lightning has begun to move on: heading perhaps for another city, some place way beyond. Even so, it's still a dark and dangerous place to be at this time of night.

Anything can happen, without warning, which is exactly what occurs across at City Hall, when the lobby's glass panelling explodes outwards. You could be looking at a stone hitting water but with jagged shards instead of spray and some kid on a skateboard at the heart of it all. He clears the shards and then the steps, but doesn't stop there: cutting through puddles of wet neon until he's out of sight, safe from harm, and with a disk burning holes in his pocket.

Figures stumble from the shattered opening: three guards and a man dressed up like some kind of Samurai cowboy. The bad combination of hat and gown is the least of his problems, however, given the battering he appears to have taken and the inside information in the boy's possession.

'Where's the limo?' he barks. 'Goddamn, why isn't it waiting here for me?'

Nervously, one guard steps forward and says: 'Your son instructed the chauffeur to take him to the rodeo ring.'

'*What?*'

'He's gone there with his friends. I guess he figured you wouldn't be leaving for home until later.'

'He had no right!'

'But sir,' the guard says weakly. 'With all due respect, Jack Junior can be a very difficult young man to reason with.'

Marshal J Dawe opens his mouth to demand a vehicle right here and now, but something stops him going any further. He can't even find it in himself to defend his son or sack the guards for letting him down like this. Everything has turned against him since the storm broke, and this is perhaps the final straw. Pathetically, he jabs the air with one finger, but no words follow to explain himself. He can't exactly hail a cab dressed like this, and even if he did where would he find the boy in a city this big? All he's doing is getting wet in this accursed rain, and his nose hurts like a mother. That's when the Marshal grabs the soggy hat from his head and stamps on it like a bug in need of squashing.

'Get out my way!' He storms into the lobby once more, hating himself yet more for the way he's feeling right now. *'I need a drink!'*

nineteen

When Benjamin Three-Sixty awakes, he is pleased to see his hopes have come true. The sun is shining on a brand new day, coming through the gaps that pepper this shack of his, and the air is so fresh that for once it feels good to breathe in.

The dreadlocked DJ is just a bag of bones. He's wearing boxers and a string vest, with a nickel dog tag on a chain around his neck that rattles as he rises to his feet. He could seriously use some trousers, but dressing is not a priority just now.

As always, the first thing Ben does is shuffle from the shack's back room and settle himself in front of the decks. There, he checks that the tape from his extensive library under the mixing desk has another half hour left to run. This gives him enough time to throw on some more clothes, bind those ropes of hair away from his face and soak up the sun from his stoop. He smiles to himself as he heads for the stove to cook up some coffee. Some of the kids round here who tuned into CHANNEL ZERO swore the man graced the airwaves every minute of the day.

How did they think he did it? Some kind of extraordinary special gift? Boy, it was a shame that kind of imagination faded with age. Much as he'd like to oblige, and go without sleep forever more, it would take a new, improved kind of human being to do it – the stuff of fairy tales, myth and legend . . .

Ben has to blink on opening the door, let his eyes adjust to the fierce light. It's early still. The sun has only just begun to lift into the East, but it glistens off every blade of grass and broken bottle out there in the wasteland. He carries his mug of coffee to the rocker, eases in carefully as the speakers inside the shack shake out some old school Jamaican ska. Yeah. That's nice. A rock-steady beat that's laid-back like this city should be on such a beautiful morning.

A minute passes before Benjamin Three-Sixty realises that he has company.

Across the rooftop, there's a lad on the edge. He's facing the city side, just sitting there with his legs slung over the lip of the building. With his hoodie up and his shoulders slumped, he cuts a forlorn figure, and Benjamin's first instinct is that he's about to witness a jumper. It's never happened before, but he always figured it would only be a matter of time, what with the pressures some of these young folk came under. Then he spies the board the boy is using to sit on, and breathes a big sigh of relief. For no matter what this one is going through, there's always someone watching over him.

Jude doesn't stir when the old man appears at his side. Not even a blink when he speaks.

'You know what?' Ben begins. 'When the sun comes up in the morning, this is the finest place you can be.'

Jude continues to gaze at the scrapers in the distance. Already the city is beginning to shimmer in the heat. Finally, he says, 'All these years, I never thought my father's stories might be true. Why didn't you tell me, Ben?'

Benjamin has to think about this, and joins the boy at the ledge. Like Jude, he doesn't seem worried by the drop. They could be sitting on a park bench, in fact. 'You'd never have believed me,' he says finally, 'like you didn't believe your daddy. I knew there'd be a time when you found out for yourself, and now that time has come.' He turns to face the boy. 'So, how does it feel?' he asks. 'Knowing what kind of man you're growing up to be?'

Jude reflects on his overnight adventure, all the heart-stopping feats he's pulled off. 'Dunno,' he says with a shrug. 'Does it mean I'm destined to become a drunk as well?'

'One of the good things about growing up,' says Ben, 'is that you get to see what mistakes people make, and learn from them. Your daddy ran away from his problems and that just made things worse for everyone, but it doesn't have to be that way for you. Take what he left behind. The way you, Sam and your mum have coped so well, I'd say *you're* the superheroes here.'

Now Jude turns, and holds his gaze for a beat. 'Are you going to tell me what happened to him? Maybe then I can move on with my life.'

Benjamin licks his lips, as if sizing up the right words, but then something way below steals his attention. Jude follows his line of vision, out towards the tatty street that leads to The Projects. There, he sees a motorcade of tipper trucks and bulldozers crawling past the launderette with all the weeds on top of it.

'Cactus Industries!' Jude takes a sharp intake of breath. 'Oh, Ben, I got so caught up in myself I totally forgot about the wasteland.' He snaps to his feet and grabs the board, looking torn between two things now. 'I'll be right back, OK?'

Benjamin bows his head, smiling to himself as the boy dashes across the concrete roof. *Sure thing*, he thinks, looking around his world here, wondering how this story might end.

Marvin has been busy these last few hours. So too has his cousin, Tiny Ti, but in a very different way to Jude. Right now, they're standing in front of the padlocked gates between The Projects and the wasteland – the pair of them holding placards striped by protest slogans. '*Freedom to skate!'* reads the big guy's. *'Out of bounds to builders!'* is the message Tiny Ti is struggling to hold up alone.

Even little Sam has joined them: no placard, just a passion to make his presence count. He knows Jude hasn't been home all night, but figured it was a good idea to tell his mum he'd seen his older brother leave for school early. One day, Jude will realise that he isn't just a dumb kid any more, and maybe this will prove it. Meantime, Spinner and his buddy Crash are standing just ahead of their friends. With their arms crossed high over their chests, the pair bust some kind of homeboy hand signal nobody else understands. It's a stance they've been practising for some time – hoping to look street-tuff, even if they come across more like prats-in-hats.

'Eyes up!' growls Marvin, and weighs his placard like he's about to swat some giant fly. 'Here they come!'

'Wait for me, guys!' This is Katya, pounding across the tarmac now to join her friends. She has no placard, just her laptop under one arm. Even so, with no sign of Jude it's about as useful as Crash and Spinner's stance. 'Has anyone seen him?' she asks anxiously, but nobody is listening because the first bulldozer has just rounded the block. It moves at a crawl, coughing out exhaust fumes. By the time the full convoy has come to a halt, their path blocked by the crew, a dark and pungent wreath has come to hang over the scene.

'I'm really worried,' she continues, joining Marvin and his cousin. 'His mobile's been switched off since I last heard from him.'

'Oi! Kids! *Move!*' The guy behind the wheel up there looks none too happy. He's meaty-looking, too, and even though Spinner and Crash look set to back down it's little Sam who takes the stage now: stepping up to cross his arms just as they have.

'Stay cool,' growls Marvin, but even he can't see how they're going to hold out for much longer.

'Fellas, if you don't shift out of the way, I swear I'm gonna come out of this cab and pile you up on the side so we can pass.'

'Then you'll have to start with me.'

The challenge comes out of nowhere, causing the crew and even the driver up front to look around for the source.

What they see is a boy on a board, rolling casually along the gap between the convoy and the verge. He seems to be in no particular hurry. Just enjoying this moment in the sunshine.

'*Jude!*'

He joins his friends in front of the bulldozer's giant grille, steps off to stand square with Spinner, Crash and his brave little brother. His presence is enough to persuade the others to step forward, and stand together as one.

'Where have you been?' whispers Kat, without taking her eye off the driver.

'I had to find myself.' Jude shrugs. He doesn't know what else to say.

She glances at him now, her lip curled into a dry smile. 'Oh, you're so deep. They should name an ocean after you.'

Jude ignores the jibe, for the driver seems set to live up to his threat, and flings open the door to the cab. 'So you're gonna stop me, pipsqueak? With what?'

The boy ferrets around in the pocket of his combats. At first he looks panicked, but then flashes a grin for his friends and pulls out the disk.

'Is that what I think it is?' Kat is already reaching to unzip her laptop from its case.

By now the guy from the bulldozer has been joined by other men. All of them wear hard hats and harder scowls. Looking at these hired thugs, Jude doesn't think this little square of plastic is going to frighten them away, especially not the lead driver – who rolls up his sleeves like this is work that could get messy.

'Stop right there! You can leave the lad to me.'

This time the command comes from directly behind the gang. They turn and part on instinct for a broad figure in a tasselled suit and shoestring tie. He's sporting a plaster across the bridge of his nose, and bruising to his brow. Way behind him, in The Projects car park, a limo with darkened windows purrs obediently like a pet instructed to heel. The only thing missing from the man is his ten-gallon hat, which is mostly why everyone present greets Marshal J Dawe with stunned silence.

Only Katya doesn't seem as awestruck by his balding dome, for she's crouched up against the buckled fence now, pecking at her keyboard. 'Well, well,' she says, in mock astonishment, and addresses the demolition gang. 'Did you lot know that the guy who stands to profit from your work here is about, ooh, seventeen years old, with a bad attitude, bad hair – which must run in the family – and a *really* bad name, too: Jack Junior? How embarrassing! It's no surprise he goes by the name of Mister Junior when it comes to the paperwork.' She rises to her feet now, saving her last line for the Marshal. 'What kind of father could set his son up like that? And I'm not just talking about a stupid name—'

'That's *enough*!' Marshal J Dawe shows her his palm, his face turning crimson from the neck up. 'What is it that you want?'

Katya glances over her shoulder, drawing his attention to the wasteland beyond. 'See some of those wild flowers? Over there,' she says, pointing now. 'That lovely blue spray growing all around the rusty fridge? That's cranesbill. Every year it blooms like that, doesn't matter what kind of weather.' She returns to level with him once more. 'Now that's our kind of recycling plant, Marshal Dawe, *sir*. In a place we call home.'

The Marshal reads her face for a moment. He looks set to erupt once again, but then steps back with a sigh. Finally, to the delight of the crew, he orders his men out of here. No questions. *Let's ride!*

Marvin glances at Crash, amused by this make-believe cowboy hitting his very own trail. For a moment, the air is filled with the clanking of gears as the vehicles attempt to find reverse, and once again fumes choke the air.

The Marshal oversees the retreat in silence, his back turned to Jude and his friends. He follows the last bulldozer, walking slowly behind it like these are cattle he's herding. Where the track leads on to the car lot surrounding the three tower blocks, he stops and looks over his shoulder. There's only one person he wants a good look at, as if perhaps he knows he might see him again. The way Dawe smiles to himself before swaggering back to the car, it's clear to Jude that next time he'll be ready.

twenty

The kid from the newspaper can't believe his luck. The night just gone he arrives home late, drenched from all the rain so that even his notebook is ruined, and what happens? His mum grounds him. You should've phoned, she says, not listening when he pleads that he had no money. Anything could've happened, she'd gone on to scream, before hugging him to within an inch of his life. He could've been mugged, even *murdered*!

As a result, not only has he lost all his notes from his interview with the Marshal, but from now on he's expected to come straight home from school every day, with no more newspaper work until he's shown that he can be trusted.

So he wakes up this morning, hating his life here in The Projects, and what does he find going on under his nose but a serious-looking stand-off involving that skateboarding posse from the neighbourhood and Marshal Dawe. It's all happening, right down there in front of the buckled fence! The view from his bedroom window gives him plenty of scope for some great photos. All he needs now is the story to go with it. That way, when the next edition of the paper comes out his mum will be forced to eat her words. Having fired off some killer shots he rushes to get dressed, throws on anything, it doesn't matter what, so long as he's got a fresh notebook and pen.

For a moment, not one crew member moves or even speaks a word. It's as if perhaps they're dreaming all this and don't want to risk waking up. Then Jude senses someone move beside him. A hand finds his own, meshing with his fingers.

'Tell me you tagged the Marshal's monitor before you left,' she asks quietly, 'and I'll love you forever.'

Jude looks a little startled, and not just because he's holding Kat's hand. Still, he's relieved to see a mischievous glint in her eye as the rest of the crew awaits his answer. 'OK, I forgot the tag,' he admits, weathering their groans. 'But I don't think the Marshal will forget us in a hurry.'

'Man, who cares?' Spinner unfolds his arms, and throws his hands in the air. 'You did it!'

The crew take this as their cue for the celebrations to begin, with Jude right at the heart of it. He's exhausted, but it doesn't stop him feeling really good about himself: confident with Kat and unconcerned about whether his voice might go mouse-like at the wrong moment. These changes he's been going through, and the uncertainty they've caused him, all seem worth it for this moment.

'*We* did it,' he beams, watching Marvin bear-hug his cousin, and then grinning as Spinner and Crash swap high fives.

'So come on, Jude.' This is Tiny Ti who asks the question they're all dying to know. 'Tell us how you got the disk.'

One by one they push for details, but Jude remains tight-lipped. He can barely believe he's pulled it off himself, so he can't expect the others to buy it, too.

The convoy edges between the blocks now, taking all the noise and fumes with it. A tranquil silence falls upon the crew, but it doesn't last long. For as the last of the bulldozers chug out of sight, so a new threat fans around it. Even from so far away, the crew begin to brace themselves for what is coming: rollerbladers by the dozen, with menace in their faces and mayhem in mind.

'Hey!' says Marvin. 'It's our friends from the West.'

'C'mon!' yells Spinner. 'Let's finish this!'

The crew scramble for their boards, and even Sam looks set to cut his teeth. Two of them hang back, however. A couple who have a little unfinished business of their own.

'About that date,' says Jude, as everyone else rushes towards the blocks. 'How are you fixed after school?'

'That depends,' says Kat, matching his smile. 'I've been blown out once, and if it happens again I'll have to kill you.'

'No chance of that,' Jude replies, enjoying the joke as

much as she does. 'Unless, of course, you just want to hang out on the wasteland, catch up on lost skating time.'

'We've got all the time in the world for that.' Rocking on to her tiptoes now, she kisses him lightly on the lips. 'Sometimes in life, skating has to come second.'

His heart soars when she says this, and he welcomes her arms around him. It feels good, and for a moment they remain locked like this. Across the concrete, over by the bin pen, there's a serious skirmish kicking off, but the others seem to be handling themselves just fine.

Jude glances at the block with the shack on top of it, sees a lone figure at the edge, watching over them. He smiles at Ben, forms the words '*Thank you*', even though he doubts Ben can lip-read from that distance. And then he sees something that changes his expression instantly. He freezes in Kat's embrace, his eyes widening with his mouth.

For Benjamin Three-Sixty has been joined by another figure.

The man steps up to the edge. There, he stands shoulder to shoulder with the pirate DJ, who doesn't seem surprised by his presence one little bit. Jude is too far away to recognise him by his face, but that long duffle coat he's wearing convinces him that he's looking at someone very special. It seems to hang from his shoulders, while the back of it billows and flaps in the ever-present breeze off the wasteland. From where Jude is standing, it could almost be a cape.

'Guys, this is unreal! Can I get an exclusive interview?'

Jude looks down from the block to see the kid from the newspaper trotting towards them. He's so excited he can't get the top off his pen without it pinging behind some dandelions.

Jude looks back at the summit of the block, in half a mind to make his excuses and sprint for the elevator, but where two men had been standing, now there is only one. Not a superhero, but a guy in the twilight of his years with an eternal passion for pirate radio. A man that he could almost call his father. He smiles to himself, imagines Ben doing likewise. He doesn't feel angry or elated, just an overwhelming sense of understanding and acceptance.

'So, what happened?' The kid is wearing sunglasses this morning, but he can barely keep them on the bridge of his nose. He pushes them up as he prepares to write, but they only slip forward again. 'Let's go right back to the beginning,' he says, giving up on looking cool, 'when you first heard that the Marshal had plans to profit from the wasteland.'

He's standing right in front of the pair now, but from what Jude can see over his shoulder it seems he's missed out on a memorable turf war. The last time he looked it was chaos – bladers and skaters everywhere – and now there's nothing at all. Jude struggles not to chuckle to himself in case the kid with all the questions takes offence. Still, he can just imagine how those daisies from the West turned tail when big Marvin bore down on them. What's more, the scattered hoots and distant cries suggest his crew is still giving chase.

'C'mon, Jude,' the kid persists. 'Gimme all the dirt you can. A scoop this big is my ticket outta here.'

'Where else would you want to go?' Jude invites him to look around. The sun has turned every open window in the tower blocks to gold, and swallows are flitting over the wasteland. Even the moon has stayed out for the occasion, pale and tissue-thin in the blue skies above the blocks. The kid faces back to Jude, takes another good look around. 'This place is *it.*'

The kid shrugs, but can't argue with that. 'I'd still like to run the story, though. You guys are gonna love some of the shots I took just now. I got your best sides, too!'

Kat glances at Jude. On his nod, she steps forward to collect the boy's camera: lifting it away from his chest and over his head. Before he's even drawn breath to protest, she strips out the film and shows it to the sun.

'What are you doing? That film's ruined now!'

'Under the circumstances,' she says, 'it might be best if we all pretend this never happened. The Marshal is a powerful man. He'll slip out of this one no sweat. Doesn't matter what you write, he'll turn it on us and we don't want any more grief. We only won a battle here today,' she finishes, 'but we can't win the war without working together.'

The kid from the newspaper looks crestfallen. His big break, too!

'Your moment will come,' Jude says to reassure him. 'It happens to us all, normally when we're not expecting it. Let's just say if you're face starts to go shiny, be ready.'

The kid seems confused, though it serves to make Kat giggle. What clears it up for him is the way Jude really does seem to float on air as he heads off with the girl at his side. Man, he looks like a dude who just got what he always wanted. And if it really does happen to everyone, like the boy with the board just said, then he's in for the time of his life!

I genuinely believed I was a
superhero, but only for a weekend.
My mum agreed to stitch together a mask
made from an old pair of jeans, and I have
a clear memory of what the local high
street looked like through the denim eyeholes.
I retired early, having realised I only had the
power to make people laugh. Still, I got something
out of it - and that was the spark
for this story.

Matt Whyman is also the author of XY.

FESTIVAL

David Belbin

The Glastonbury Festival. Three days in June. For many, it's the event of the summer – for three Glastonbury virgins and one fourteen-year-old veteran, it's going to be a life-changing experience.

Leila, exams over, just wants to have fun. But first she has to find a way to get there . . .

Jake is playing the festival. This could be his big break. Or his biggest nightmare . . .

Wilf is forced to sell his ticket, so his only way in is to jump the fence. And there's a big surprise waiting on the other side . . .

Holly gets in free. It's her tenth Glastonbury. She's promised herself it'll be the last . . .

NOSTRADAMUS AND INSTANT NOODLES

John Larkin

Ian Champion's mum and dad came to parenthood late – and by accident. It wasn't a good start and now – fourteen years later – his parents have had enough.

Suddenly from Sydney and its sun, sand and surf, Ian finds himself staying with relatives in chilly Yorkshire, faced with football, flatcaps and flooding.

This is what happens when your parents leave home before you do . . .